7-04

THE China War
AND THE
Third Temple

IRVIN BAXTER

THE China War AND THE Third Temple

Destiny Image Fiction

An Imprint of

Destiny Image® Publishers, Inc.
P.O. Box 310
Shippensburg, PA 17257-0310

ISBN 0-7684-3043-7

For Worldwide Distribution
Printed in the U.S.A.

This book and all other Destiny Image, Revival Press, MercyPlace, Fresh Bread, Destiny Image Fiction, and Treasure House books are available at Christian bookstores and distributors worldwide.

For a U.S. bookstore nearest you, call **1-800-722-6774**.
For more information on foreign distributors, call **717-532-3040**.
Or reach us on the Internet: **www.destinyimage.com**

Dedication

To my wonderful parents who
recently entered eternal life;
To the wonderful congregation
at Oak Park Church that I pastor;
To my precious girls—Karla, Kara and Jana;
And to my wonderful wife and partner, Judy.

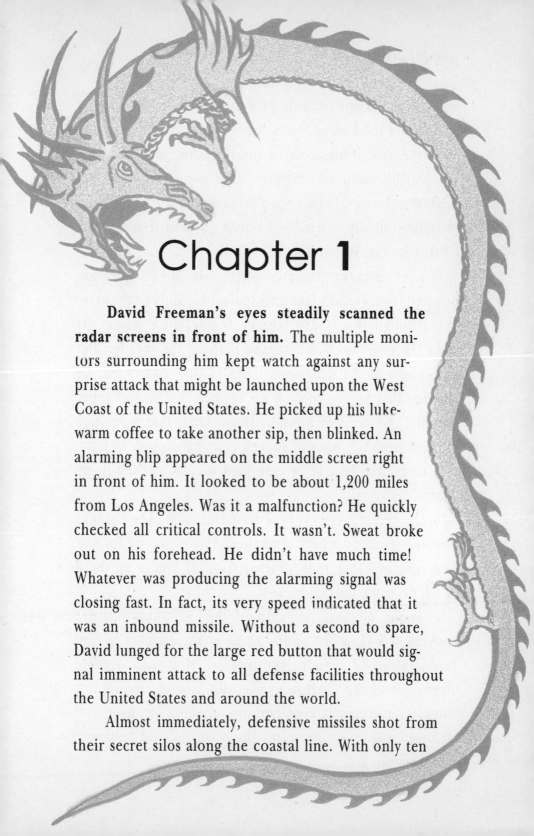

Chapter 1

David Freeman's eyes steadily scanned the radar screens in front of him. The multiple monitors surrounding him kept watch against any surprise attack that might be launched upon the West Coast of the United States. He picked up his lukewarm coffee to take another sip, then blinked. An alarming blip appeared on the middle screen right in front of him. It looked to be about 1,200 miles from Los Angeles. Was it a malfunction? He quickly checked all critical controls. It wasn't. Sweat broke out on his forehead. He didn't have much time! Whatever was producing the alarming signal was closing fast. In fact, its very speed indicated that it was an inbound missile. Without a second to spare, David lunged for the large red button that would signal imminent attack to all defense facilities throughout the United States and around the world.

Almost immediately, defensive missiles shot from their secret silos along the coastal line. With only ten

THE China War

minutes remaining until the incoming weapon released its payload on the United States, the U.S. Defense Forces had only one shot at intercepting the intruding missile. David watched his radar screen with bated breath as the newly deployed Arrow Missiles sped toward the invader. If the incoming missile carried a nuclear payload, David knew what it meant: World War III!

The next two minutes were critical. Perspiration dripped from David's face and soaked his shirt to the skin, even though the control center temperature was at its usual 72 degrees. Watching the path of the invader and the course of the defense missiles as they converged, he realized that he was holding his breath. "Relax, stay calm, breathe," he ordered himself. David knew that if he ever implemented the years of special training on how to function under the heat of intense pressure, he needed to do it now!

His eyes tracked every blip on the radar. The defense missiles seemed to have a chance! David prayed for the first time in a long time. "Please, God. If You're up there at all, do something right now."

At the moment the path of the defending missiles converged with the incoming route of the attacker, a confusing array of signals appeared on the radar screen. Then, out of the confusion, the blip moving toward Los Angeles emerged. It kept coming, growing stronger and stronger with every pulse on the screen. "God help us!" David cried.

2

Even though the control center was built to withstand a direct nuclear hit, David still felt the shudder and heard the deep beastly rumble as the nuclear explosion unleashed all of its fury on the heart of downtown L.A. An urgent message went out to all U.S. defense facilities around the world: "The United States has sustained a full nuclear attack on its western coast. Millions are undoubtedly dead in the Los Angeles area. Most likely origin of the attack—China."

Over the next 20 minutes, beneath the pandemonium above, radar records of all areas of the Pacific were reviewed carefully. It was concluded that the attack must have originated from a Chinese submarine reported to have been in the area earlier that day.

U.S. President Benton picked up the red hotline phone connecting him directly to China's president. On the other end he heard, "Hello."

"Mr. President, what is going on?" President Benton almost shouted.

"President Benton, we told you that if you interfered with our rightful claims to the Island of Taiwan, there would be a terrible price to pay. Apparently you didn't believe us. You will suffer no more attacks if you withdraw your troops from the Straits of Taiwan. And stay out of Chinese business." Click.

When members of the Chinese foreign ministry had delivered threats to the U.S. State Department of just this kind of action in 1996, Bill Clinton, who was President at the time, had thought surely that they were bluffing. Obviously, they weren't.

Momentarily stunned, President Benton knew there was no time to waste. Contingency plans had been created for just this scenario. It was obvious to all in the State Department that a conventional war with 1.3 billion Chinese was out of the question. If Chinese aggression was not stopped here and now, they would soon rule the entire globe.

The President, with set jaw, looked over at the ever-present military officer with the black box. With every eye in the underground room watching, he ordered, "Open it—quick!" The officer's hands shook with the understanding of the import of his actions. But he never hesitated. Within ten minutes of the devastation of L.A., a full nuclear attack was unleashed upon the People's Republic of China. As ghastly as this course of action was, the President knew it was his only recourse. Within 30 minutes, Red China, for all practical purposes, would cease to exist.

The powers in China had known there might be retaliation, but they had not anticipated what they saw moving at mach-17 speed toward their beloved mainland. The radar screens that kept watch over China's skies were absolutely filled with the incoming retaliatory missiles of the United States. And there was nothing they could do to stop them!

Chinese President Zhiang stared at Premier Cho. "You said America would back down!" he screamed accusingly. "Look at what you've done!"

Cho shot back, "Our sources have never misled us before. Something has gone terribly wrong! Mr. President, make those U.S. devils pay! You must immediately order a counterstrike. We owe it to the memory of the Chinese people!"

Zhiang picked up the military command phone. The ranking military officer answered immediately. "Yes, Mr. President."

"Do we have time to launch every nuclear missile that we have before America's weapons reach the motherland?" Zhiang asked. China had redirected every nuclear weapon in her arsenal toward America when tensions over Taiwan had begun to heat up.

The officer hesitated. "Mr. President, I'm not sure. It will be very close."

"Then do it now!" Zhiang shouted. He heard the phone slam onto the receiver as the military officer ran to execute his leader's command.

5

President Zhiang approached the array of screens monitoring the global theater of war. "Will our missiles be launched in time?" he asked.

The communications officer's eyes scanned the dials monitoring the operation of every missile. "We don't know yet, sir. It's too close to call."

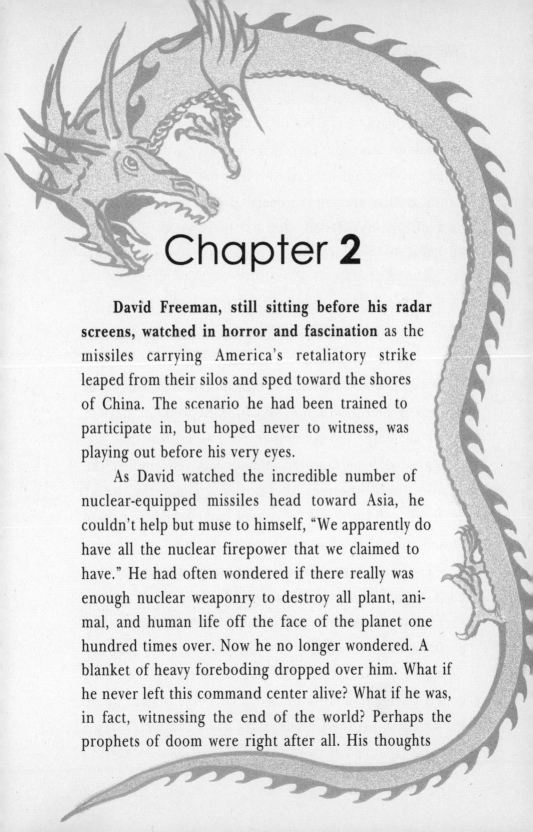

Chapter 2

David Freeman, still sitting before his radar screens, watched in horror and fascination as the missiles carrying America's retaliatory strike leaped from their silos and sped toward the shores of China. The scenario he had been trained to participate in, but hoped never to witness, was playing out before his very eyes.

As David watched the incredible number of nuclear-equipped missiles head toward Asia, he couldn't help but muse to himself, "We apparently do have all the nuclear firepower that we claimed to have." He had often wondered if there really was enough nuclear weaponry to destroy all plant, animal, and human life off the face of the planet one hundred times over. Now he no longer wondered. A blanket of heavy foreboding dropped over him. What if he never left this command center alive? What if he was, in fact, witnessing the end of the world? Perhaps the prophets of doom were right after all. His thoughts raced. Would he ever see his beautiful wife Sharon again? His little black-haired boy, David Jr., was four years old. What about him? And then there was Misty, that gorgeous blond two-year-old darling who had her fingers wrapped tightly around her daddy's heart. Hot tears burned at the back of his eyes. "David, stop it!" he shouted to himself. Such was the tension and emotion in the room that no one else noticed his cry.

David mentally yanked himself back to his senses. "Pull yourself together, Freeman," he muttered. His eyes once again began to scan the screens for additional incoming attacks. Once America's three hundred missiles had unleashed their destruction on China, he wouldn't have to worry anymore. But until then, it was critical that any enemy missiles be detected immediately. The sooner the missiles were spotted, the better chance the newly deployed defensive missile system had of bringing them down before they could reach their targets.

The most disturbing thought of all now presented itself to his mind. What about Russia? Would Russia decide to defend China? Or would she think this was the optimum time to destroy the U.S.—clearing the way for Russian domination of the 21st Century? He certainly hoped such a foolhardy thing would never occur. Surely Russia knew that the United States had a completely separate arsenal aimed at its principal nuclear rival on earth.

Time passed slowly, inevitably. In ten minutes the destruction of China would be an accomplished fact. David found himself filled with exultation at what he knew was within his country's grasp.

But then his thoughts roamed to the human aspect of war. In his mind he could see little children running on the playgrounds and streets of China. He saw young fathers and nursing mothers. He saw grandparents proudly holding their grand-babies. All of a sudden, the absolute horror of what man was unleashing upon his fellowman hit him in the gut. "Oh my God!" he exclaimed. "How could this ever have happened?!"

Three minutes, two minutes, one minute... David watched as the missiles swept downward toward their targets. First hit was Canton, then Shanghai, Tianjin, Shenyang, Guangzhou—every one of China's major cities—and finally Beijing.

The live broadcast feed from China, shown at the other end of the control room, continued to report developments as the first few nuclear explosions unleashed their death-dealing fury on the Chinese populace. Little did these broadcasters suspect that they themselves would, within minutes, be swallowed up within a raging nuclear inferno. But as he listened, David understood it completely. "Oh my God," David said to himself. "Oh my God!"

When the last missile struck its target, David sat back and sighed. *This war is over!* Still, he decided to scan the screens one more time—just in case. On his final pass, what he saw turned his blood to ice water in his veins. "Oh no! My God, no!" He counted five, no, seven, there's three more, twelve, thirteen...thirteen nuclear warheads headed toward the United States! "Those Chinese! They knew they were going down, so they decided to take the U.S. down with them!"

David rapidly typed into the computer. Almost instantly his message appeared on every defense center's computer screen in America.

"URGENT! RED ALERT! Thirteen incoming nuclear missiles from China. All anti-missile weapons must be deployed immediately! I repeat. All anti-missile weapons must be deployed immediately! URGENT! RED ALERT!"

David sat back again, knowing he had done his job. He had done all he could do for the time being. About that time, next to his screens, the red phone reserved for top secret military communications rang. "Officer David Freeman here," he answered.

The voice on the other end stated crisply, "Please hold for the President of the United States."

David barely had time to catch his breath.

The President moved straight to the point. "Is this the L.A. Defense Center?"

"It is, sir," David replied.

"Are you the officer who sent the initial warning of China's pending attack?" President Benton asked.

"Affirmative, sir," David answered.

The President continued, "I have just received a report of thirteen nuclear missiles incoming from China. Is this report true?"

"Yes, sir. That is true," David responded.

"Officer Freeman, are we sure these new missiles are not coming from Russia or another enemy nation?" President Benton inquired. "It's urgent that I know for sure immediately!"

"Mr. President, I was watching the screens, monitoring the coast of China. I thought we had successfully caught the enemy's missiles on the ground. But just as our missiles began to hit their targets, I decided I should take one more look as a precaution. That's when I saw China's missiles rise from their silos. I'm sorry, sir."

"Thank you very much, officer. Good job. Remain at your post of duty and stay alert. This may not be over yet!" The President hung up without saying good-bye.

David had no time to reflect on the implications of what had just transpired. He had spoken directly to the President of the United States during an historic military conflict. There would be time later to contemplate the role into which he had been thrust in this momentous contest. Right now there were millions of American lives to be saved.

He focused his attention on the screens displaying the frightening array of missiles—both incoming and outgoing. David felt sure that the 13 missiles fired by China would be her last. Even now he knew that China was no more. But those nuclear missiles were very real and deadly beyond imagination. They had to be stopped! What were their targets? New York? San Diego? Denver? Washington, D.C.? Houston? Chicago? No one knew for sure. Only one thing was certain. Those nuclear missiles represented vengeance, the vengeance of the Red Chinese Dragon. Shudders ran up and down David's spine at the thought.

Events were happening one after another at incredible speed, but David felt like he was watching everything in slow motion. His eyes followed the Chinese missiles on the screen as they sped toward their predetermined targets—targets that remained a mystery to the intended victims.

Most Americans were aware by now that L.A. had been hit and that war was on. However, few understood that millions of them could be incinerated into nothingness within the next 30 minutes. "If only we had built that Star Wars missile defense system when President Reagan wanted to!" David mused. "We would have perfected it by now, and none of this would be happening."

As David watched the first battery of anti-missile weapons converge upon the leading Chinese warheads, he found himself holding his breath again. As the U.S. signals and the enemy signals intersected, David again prayed. "God, please help." The massive explosion he saw on the monitor indicated a direct hit. "Yes!" he cried.

The U.S. missiles converged on Chinese warhead number two. Again, the explosion on the screen indicated success. "All right!" David's optimism was growing. Maybe with enough notice, these Arrow Missiles could be effective.

Just when David was starting to breathe easier about the situation, the third missile slipped through the defenses. *Oh God, I wonder where that one is headed?* he thought to himself. The fourth nuclear missile slipped through as well. "C'mon, God," David cried. "You've got to help us!"

Two of the U.S. missiles converged at once on Chinese missile number five. The resulting explosion told David it was a direct hit. Missile number six continued past the missile shield, as did seven and eight. Five Chinese missiles had slipped through! Then number nine was hit. Ten kept coming, and number eleven slipped through as well. *This isn't going very well*, David thought to himself. *The Chinese knew our defense system was not reliable yet. That's probably the reason they decided to push the Taiwan issue now instead of later.*

Three anti-missile weapons blasted Chinese missile number twelve out of the sky, but number thirteen made it through. David counted...one, two, three, four, five, six, seven, eight. Eight missiles in all made it through. Eight of America's cities would soon go up in flames...nuclear flames.

David realized his job was not over yet. He needed to send warnings as soon as he figured out which cities were to be hit. He watched closely as missile number three began its deadly descent. It appeared to be headed for Denver. David sent an alert, but they had less than five minutes left. He turned away to track the next one.

His eyes narrowed as missile number four continued on to the southern part of the United States. The trajectory told David that Houston was the likely target. He had friends in Houston. Four minutes later, his fears were confirmed. *I wonder if Jim and Katie are home right now?* Again, he turned his attention away.

Missile number six had begun its dive much more quickly. Three minutes later it became obvious that Chicago was about to be history.

Things were happening so fast now that everything depended on instinct. Missile seven swept toward Phoenix. Missile number eight sped toward Charlotte, North Carolina. Then number ten dove downward into the heart of Boston.

Two to go, David counted to himself. Missile number 11 headed southwest. "Where is that going?" David wondered aloud. He didn't have to wonder long. When it reached the border of Georgia, it swept downward like a deadly serpent into the center of Atlanta.

The last Chinese missile sped toward its target. David feared that he knew its destination. He could only hope that Washington, D.C. had been targeted by one of the downed nuclear warheads. But it wasn't to be. Swiftly and surely, the long, sleek, powerful missile arched downward.

David grimaced when the explosion ripped through the capital of the United States. The Senate was gone. The House of Representatives was gone. The White House was no more.

The radar screens were empty now.

But what about President Benton? David knew that he should be somewhere in Air Force One—the mobile command center of the United States. This President, who had wanted so badly to be known as the "Peace President," would instead be linked eternally to the worst slaughter ever unleashed upon the human race.

"It's not time to relax yet," David reminded himself. "Too many things could still spin out of control." Of course, the foremost concern was Russia with her massive and still lethal nuclear arsenal. His eyes continued to scan the radar screens that watched the Russian frontier. Every minute that passed, without sign of activity from that front, increased the likelihood that the war would not widen.

David knew that the U.S. President was probably at this moment on the red hotline phone with the Russian President, delivering assurances that this catastrophe had occurred only because of China's nuclear attack on Los Angeles. He was sure that President Benton was already explaining that the United States had no desire to attack Russia or any other country.

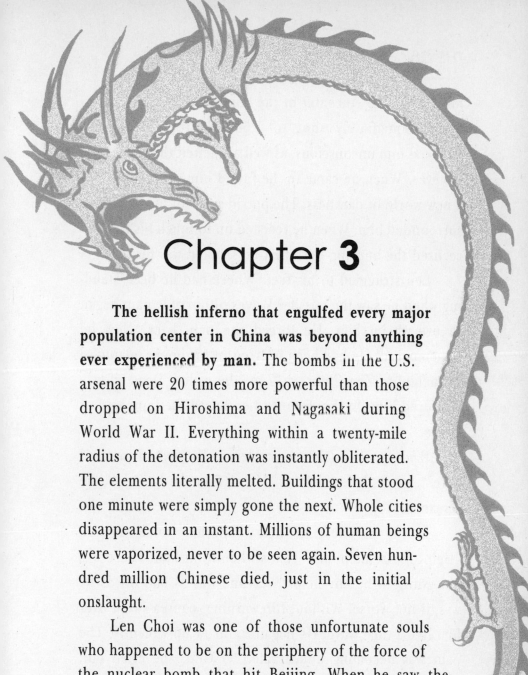

Chapter 3

The hellish inferno that engulfed every major population center in China was beyond anything ever experienced by man. The bombs in the U.S. arsenal were 20 times more powerful than those dropped on Hiroshima and Nagasaki during World War II. Everything within a twenty-mile radius of the detonation was instantly obliterated. The elements literally melted. Buildings that stood one minute were simply gone the next. Whole cities disappeared in an instant. Millions of human beings were vaporized, never to be seen again. Seven hundred million Chinese died, just in the initial onslaught.

Len Choi was one of those unfortunate souls who happened to be on the periphery of the force of the nuclear bomb that hit Beijing. When he saw the incoming missile, he froze in his tracks. Before he could react at all, the power of the explosion hit with the force of a thousand freight trains. Even where Len stood 25 miles from the epicenter of the bomb's force, the temperature immediately shot to 1,500 degrees. The blast knocked him unconscious, as well as melted the corneas of his eyes. When he came to, he found himself thrown into a new world of darkness. The putrid smell of burning flesh surrounded him. When he reached up to touch his face, he realized the burning flesh that he smelled was his own.

Len struggled to his feet. Where had he been standing when he saw the missile? Waves of horrible pain began to overwhelm him. He forced the pain back. Now he remembered! He had been in front of his house talking to his neighbor Zen Chinroy. "Zen," he called. Dead silence answered him. In the distance Len heard the faint wail of sirens.

What should I do? Len wondered. "Is anybody around here?" he called. Silence. "Help! Somebody help!" he screamed.

In his darkness he heard another voice scream, "Help! Please help me!" That's when it hit him. There was not going to be any help. Everyone was as bad off as he was, if not worse. Without forewarning, nausea swept over him like a tidal wave. He began to throw up violently. The pain was becoming unbearable. "O God," he cried out. "Please help me." Len didn't know whether he believed in a God or not; their Communist leaders had told them that there was no God. But for some reason this horrible situation made the existence of God seem very real.

Five years ago, a classmate named Chang had risked his life to tell him about Jesus, but Len had made fun of him. Len now wished that he had listened.

What to do? It was too late to worry about all of that now. Len understood that he couldn't last long in this horrible condition. The never-ending pain would soon render him incapable of functioning. He knew he would die a slow, very painful death.

Len's mind went to the pistol in the drawer beside his bed. He calculated where the door of his house was. He slid his foot along the sidewalk until his toe made contact with the steps that led up to the porch. When he came to the door, the brass handle was still too hot to touch. Pulling his handkerchief from his pocket, he used it to open the door.

Len paused just inside for a moment, ignoring the pain, mentally reconstructing the layout of his home. He calculated that the stairs leading up to his bedroom were about six strides from where he stood. He had felt his way through the house many times in the dark, but it was much more difficult when you couldn't see at all.

His groping hand found the railing. Good! He had reached the staircase. He bent his knees to climb the first step—and felt his skin breaking. The pain was intense! He willed himself to take each step. He had to escape this living hell that he suddenly found himself thrown into the middle of!

Pausing at the top of the steps, he again attempted, in his new, totally dark world, to visualize the location of his bedroom. Second door on the right. No, third. He had forgotten about the bathroom door. When you can see, you never think about how many doors there are. You just go where you want to go. Things are so different in the world of the blind!

As Len entered into his bedroom, he knew that he needed to move in the direction of approximately 11 o'clock. When he took the fifth step, he felt his leg bump against the edge of his bed. Pain shot up to his hip.

He sat down on the side of the bed, pausing to regain his strength and to gather his courage. Could he go through with what he planned? Memories of his mother and dad came floating to the surface of his mind. He had no doubt about what had happened to them. They lived in downtown Beijing. They never knew what hit them. It was better for them that way.

His sister Lipeng lived out in the country with her new husband. Perhaps they had a chance of surviving. Len didn't know whether that would be good or bad. He wished he could know if she was all right, but if she wasn't, he was in no condition to help. And if she was all right, he would only be an additional burden. Had Lipeng and her husband survived, they sure didn't need a blind invalid like he was going to be burdening them down. Yes, the route he had chosen was the best for everyone. Now, if he could just find the gun.

Len groped for the drawer that he knew was there. When he tried to pull it open, his fingers slipped off the handle. At that moment, he realized that his burnt hands were bleeding. Despair swept over him as he realized how utterly hopeless his situation was. He sighed. His whole life should've been ahead of him. He'd had big plans. It wasn't supposed to end like this.

Len gripped the drawer with both hands and felt it slide open. Searching around inside, he finally felt the barrel of the Colt 45 pistol. It was one of his prized possessions. He had bought it from an American he had come to know when they both served with the UN in Bosnia.

Was the gun loaded? Len tried to remember. He had to do this right the first time, while his courage still held. He slid his finger along the barrel until he found the release that opened the cylinder. He spun the cylinder slowly, feeling for bullets. Empty! *Where did I leave those bullets? I've got to find them while I still have the strength to do this!*

"The closet! I remember now. I put them on the top shelf clear over to the left." Len felt his way along the bed until he reached the closet. Opening the door, he slid his hand along the top shelf. Finally, reaching all the way back, his fingers closed around the box containing the ammunition. In spite of himself, he felt the tears flowing down his hot, burnt cheeks at the realization of what he was about to do. Well, it didn't really matter now anyway.

Making his way back to the bedside, he thought about calling his sister to say good-bye. "Stupid," he muttered to himself. "There's no phone service left anywhere in this country." Len thought of the times he had wanted to tell his mother and dad that he loved them, but showing emotion was frowned upon by the party. It supposedly showed weakness. He wished now he had done it anyway.

The thought occurred to Len that he could lie down for a while. Maybe help would yet come from somewhere. He started to lower his head onto the pillow, but the pain wouldn't allow it. "There's no use. I've got to get this over with now. There's nothing ahead for me but pain and darkness. There's just no hope."

Len slid the bullets into the cylinder one by one. He decided to put all six in, even though he didn't intend to need but one. Maybe someone else would come along who could use the other five.

"God, I don't know You—if You're there at all. I didn't take the few opportunities that I did have to search after You. If You are there and can hear me, please forgive me. I'm sorry I've lived such a self-centered life."

With tears dripping down his cheeks and off his blackened chin, Len slid the barrel of the pistol into his mouth and quickly squeezed the trigger.

When help did arrive much, much later, the technicians were unmoved by the sight of the corpse. They had encountered numerous scenes like this one—and worse—all over China. Most of the stories were never told since members of the media knew they signed their own death warrants if they tried to go into the contaminated areas.

For several days after the initial nuclear inferno, the nuclear clouds unleashed their death-dealing rains. For most, there was no place to run, no place to hide. The unthinkable was occurring while the world looked helplessly on. It was, in reality, "hell on earth."

Special radiation units were quickly organized under UN supervision. They began to go into the less contaminated areas in an attempt to save anyone who could be saved. The results were not good. It was estimated that 10 million Chinese were dying each day. At that rate, in another 30 days, an additional 300 million Chinese would be dead! That would bring the Chinese fatalities alone to 1 billion.

The force of the nuclear attack had been greater than the United States had intended. Death was everywhere. It covered China like a heavy gray blanket. The scenes were horrific.

As fate would have it, winds swept the massive nuclear clouds toward the one billion people living in India. Individuals of means paid extortion prices to catch the few flights that were leaving India's airports. Tickets out of the country were going for $50,000 per person!

When the nuclear contaminated rains began, India's highways were immediately clogged with people attempting to flee the liquid death pouring from the sky. It did not take long for the highways to become huge clogged arteries of death. Those who had motorcycles and scooters had the best chance to outrun the invading nuclear death cloud. People would actually gauge the direction of the wind and plan their escape routes accordingly. The scooters and bicycles could be seen cutting through open fields in desperate attempts to flee the plague of death. It was as though the pale horse of the Apocalypse pursued them... and was winning.

For most, fleeing was nothing more than an exercise in futility. The rains overtook them and millions clung to each other in mortal fear as the raindrops of death streamed down their faces. Young and old, male and female, high-ranking and low-level, ran into caves, homes, stores, barns— anyplace that afforded shelter. But even if shelter was found, the pungent smell of the nuclear-infested air burned its way into their lungs. Death wouldn't come as quickly to those who only breathed the air, but it would come nevertheless.

As the massive nuclear clouds swept through India, the death toll they began to exact was tallied in the tens of millions. Satellite pictures of the course of the nuclear clouds were shown daily on television. Of course there was little, if any, on-site reporting. Broadcasters with major news services who in the past had held apocalyptic predictions in derision now wondered aloud if the plagues of the Apocalypse itself had not been unleashed. Within 90 days, the count of India's dead and dying reached 500 million.

Even as the nuclear clouds moved over India, the death toll in China continued to mount. Now the UN had a new goal: Spare enough of the Chinese race to save it from total extinction. It was that bad. The Chinese would be fortunate if 100 million of their original 1.3 billion ultimately survived.

Normally the United States would have been in the forefront of the relief efforts in China and India. Instead, the nation had more than she could handle in trying to bury her own dead and dying—some 20 million of them. Every hospital was jammed with those experiencing radiation sickness. Complicating the problem was the fact that so few doctors really knew how to treat radiation victims.

Then there was the massive job of rebuilding eight major cities, or at least of reviving what could be reclaimed out of the rubble. The federal governmental offices had been moved to Philadelphia until it could be decided where the new United States capital would be. There was no possibility of rebuilding it in Washington, D.C., since that would be a no-man's land for the next one hundred years.

Many major U.S. corporations had suffered the loss of their headquarters and their leaders. The financial losses were absolutely staggering. In effect, the United

States had been hit with a body blow that knocked her to her knees.

All across the globe, world power structures were being altered forever. China, who had been projected to dominate the 21st Century, was gone. Instead of having an India that was prepared to assume its proper role in the World Community as an emerging superpower of 1 billion people, the world now had a nation of 500 million that promised to be the "sick man" of the world for the foreseeable future.

When the full magnitude of the destruction was finally assessed, a stunned world realized that two billion human beings, one-third of the world's population, had been wiped out. The United States tried to place the blame on China, but there was no one left in China to blame. World opinion turned very ugly toward the U.S. because of the unthinkable carnage she had perpetrated upon the human race.

World news was filled with recrimination toward America. Charges of nurturing the "One China" policy, then triggering a nuclear holocaust when China tried to enforce it, flew against President Benton. One nation even accused the U.S. of deliberately planning the conflict so that China could be eliminated as a threat to U.S. leadership in the 21st Century. More and more, the media portrayed America as an imperialist state seeking to impose her will on the entire world. Overnight, U.S.

influence was greatly diminished, and the world's leadership passed to Europe and Russia.

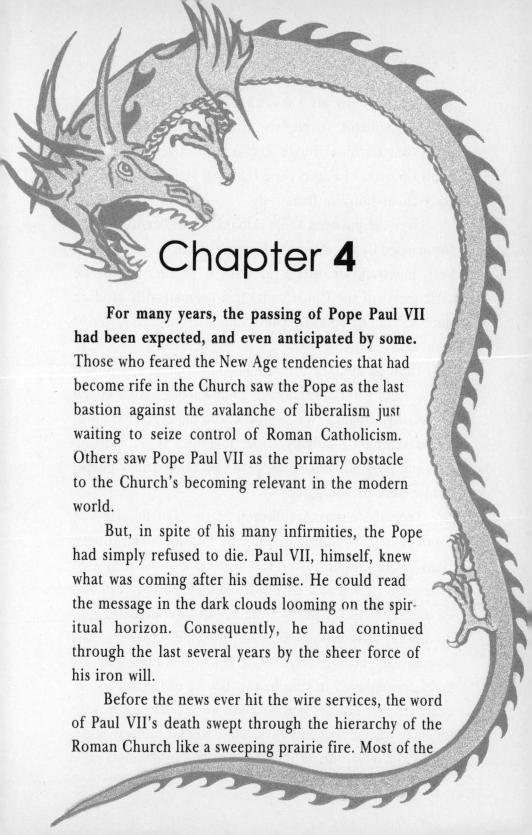

Chapter 4

For many years, the passing of Pope Paul VII had been expected, and even anticipated by some. Those who feared the New Age tendencies that had become rife in the Church saw the Pope as the last bastion against the avalanche of liberalism just waiting to seize control of Roman Catholicism. Others saw Pope Paul VII as the primary obstacle to the Church's becoming relevant in the modern world.

But, in spite of his many infirmities, the Pope had simply refused to die. Paul VII, himself, knew what was coming after his demise. He could read the message in the dark clouds looming on the spiritual horizon. Consequently, he had continued through the last several years by the sheer force of his iron will.

Before the news ever hit the wire services, the word of Paul VII's death swept through the hierarchy of the Roman Church like a sweeping prairie fire. Most of the powers-that-be already knew who would be considered as prime candidates to replace the long-reigning pontiff. There was Cardinal Binge Zingarni of Nigeria, Cardinal Louis Glouster of France, and Cardinal Marlos Lustini, the powerful archbishop from Italy.

Over the past few years, alliances had been carefully constructed by the different factions of the Church. There were the traditionalists who wanted to reestablish the basic tenets of the Church that had been steadily eroding since Vatican Council II. These rallied around Glouster of France.

Those in alliance with Zingarni of Nigeria envisioned a true world Church espousing an all-encompassing global spirituality. Zingarni was a mystic who believed that all of mankind would suddenly come together, if only distinguishing religious doctrines were laid aside and a gospel of love were promulgated.

Then there was Archbishop Marlos Lustini. He was cosmopolitan, complex, intelligent, shrewd, and ruthless. Many in the Church feared this man because he possessed what some viewed as a dark side. True, he stood head and shoulders above his peers in ability and intelligence. And his worldly connections were unparalleled. Over the past several years, many heads-of-state who visited Pope Paul VII had felt compelled to stop by the diocese of Lustini also in order to pay homage and to cultivate a relationship with this man who most believed would become the next pope, leader of almost one billion of the earth's inhabitants. The supporters of Lustini were confident that it was their man who could restore the Roman Catholic Church to its proper place of power and influence in the world.

As the Cardinals descended upon Rome for the conclave that would choose the replacement for Pope Paul VII, each one was poignantly aware that this would not be just another conclave. The world was at an unprecedented juncture. Plans for true world government had been painstakingly developed over the past one hundred years. The computerization of society had now rendered all of mankind interdependent. The United Nations was on the verge of becoming a bona fide instrument of global governance. Dreams and destinies were converging. The pope chosen in this conclave would either position the Church to sit astride the New World Order, or allow it to be swept aside by the powerful New Age Revolution that was, even now, surging throughout the bloodstream of humanity.

The sea of red was stunning to behold as the Princes of the Church slowly made their way toward the entrance of the Sistine Chapel. Once the Cardinals were all inside the building, the doors would be closed, and no one would be permitted to enter or leave until a new pope was elected.

Cardinal Cassidy from the United States was the last Cardinal to enter. The Vatican guards stood watchfully at the door while the official search party carefully inspected every area of the Sistine Chapel. No unauthorized person was allowed inside the conclave area once the balloting began. Finding nothing amiss, the head of the search party nodded to the guards. Immediately the heavy door of the Sistine Chapel was shut and the key turned in the lock. It would not be opened until the new pope was chosen.

The Cardinals moved into the chapel where the oath of secrecy and loyalty would be administered. Every part of this ritual was designed to impress upon the participants the importance of the drama that they were called upon to enact. After solemnly swearing the oath, each of the prelates moved toward the room that would serve as his living quarters until a new pope was elected.

Over dinner that night, the conversation of the prelates was animated and urgent. Every person there understood that this was no normal conclave. They had been summoned together to choose a pope who would either preside over the collapse of the Church's power, or guide the Church through the treacherous waters of the emerging New World Order and position her to play her rightful role as Mother and Teacher of the world.

The powerful Vatican Secretary-of-State, Antonio Solano, sat at his privileged table opposite the entrance of the dining hall. His shrewd eyes took in each prelate as he walked through the door. When Zingarni of Nigeria

entered, Solano's thoughts raced. Here was a man of inno-
cence, purity, and goodwill. For a kinder, gentler time, he
would have occupied the papacy quite well. But in the 21st
Century world of transition, electing him as Pope would
be like throwing a babe into a pit of snakes. Zingarni was
simply out of the question.

A few minutes later, Cardinal Glouster entered the
dining hall. Poised, intelligent, and aware, no one could
accuse Glouster of being a lightweight. But the Cardinal
was still locked into the 20th Century. Solano was sure
that he did not appreciate the power of the forces that
were running counter to the Church. For example,
Glouster was uncompromising on the birth control issue.
Yes, the Church's official position had been against birth
control for many years now. But when one billion people
were living on less than one dollar per day, the Church
simply had to come to grips with reality! Was Glouster the
man of the hour? Solano didn't think so.

When most of the Cardinals were seated at their
tables, Marlos Lustini made his entrance. Cardinal Lustini
was about five feet, nine inches tall and weighed 169
pounds. His sharp features and his piercing eyes left no
doubt that here was a man of superior intelligence and
authority.

Solano willed himself to be objective and analytical
about this man, but he found that to be almost impossible. Solano had rubbed shoulders with kings, presidents,
and prelates, but he had never met anyone with the raw

magnetism of Lustini. What was it about him? Solano noticed that he wasn't the only one affected by the presence of Cardinal Lustini. As the cardinal passed each table, hands reached out to greet him. Solano thought to himself, *This has to be our man.*

In spite of the fact that Lustini had "pope" written all over him, something about the prospect disturbed Solano at the deepest level of his being. What was it? He couldn't quite put his finger on it. Maybe he was being needlessly paranoid. Solano went over Lustini's qualifications one by one. Intelligent, well-connected, incredible leadership ability, adept at handling power and humble... Ah, that's what was bothering him! Only the most shrewd student of human character could notice that Lustini's humility was practiced and contrived. He was so skilled at hiding that fact that Solano himself had never picked up on it until now. But, as Lustini slowly made his way through the dining hall, it suddenly became obvious to Solano that a deep vein of pride and self-importance ran through the core of Lustini's character. Pride could be a real problem in any person. But in a man holding power over close to one billion human beings, that plague would be deadly!

Next morning the cardinals arose and entered the Sistine Chapel at the appointed time. Thrones for each prelate had been placed around the perimeter of the chapel. This practice was designed to impress upon each Prince of the Church that he might leave the conclave as the new occupant of Peter's throne.

After each cardinal had taken his place on his assigned throne, instructions were reviewed as to how the balloting would be conducted. Since Paul VII's papacy had been so long, many of the cardinals were participating in their first conclave.

Before the casting of the first ballot, Secretary-of-State Solano rose to offer the opening prayer. "Father God, look down upon Your Church as we attempt to select the individual whom You would choose to hold the keys of Peter at this most important time in human history. Let Your Holy Spirit guide our decisions so that Your will may be done in earth as it is in Heaven. Blessed Mary, Mother of God, intercede with Your Son, Jesus Christ, that He would reveal that person who should be His representative on earth for this hour. We request these divine favors in the name of the Father, and in the name of the Son, and in the name of the Holy Spirit. Amen."

All of the prelates replied, "Amen."

Each cardinal wrote his choice for pope on his ballot. They then, one by one, rose to bring their ballots to the front of the Sistine Chapel where they were placed in the papal ballot chalice.

The suspense that hung in the air was palpable. The future of nations and the course of human history would be dramatically altered by the outcome of this papal conclave. Most of the world did not understand the power that was invested in the man who presided over the one billion faithful. But the Princes of the Church understood it fully. They observed the influence of the papacy on a daily basis. "Whatsoever ye shall bind on earth shall be bound in heaven" was not an empty oath to those who had seen kingdoms crumble as a result of a mere decision by the Holy Father who occupied the Chair of Peter. When Winston Churchill had suggested enlisting the support of the Pope during World War II, Soviet Union leader Josef Stalin had derisively replied, "The Pope?! How many divisions does he have?" Now Stalin was dead, the Soviet Union was dissolved, and the Roman Church was as strong as ever. The power of the man who wore the title, Vicar of the Son of God, could be understood only by those who knew the network of churches, schools, hospitals, and political contacts presided over by the pope. Only those who had visited remote outposts of civilization and found the guiding hand of Catholic priests already there exerting the Church's influence knew what was at stake here. Only a priest who had sat in the confessional booth, hearing the darkest sins of governors, presidents, and kings, could understand just how far the tentacles of the Church really extended. And all of that power would soon be invested in one man, the man chosen in this conclave.

The cardinals chatted with those beside them as they waited for the ballots to be counted. When the Cardinal Chamberlain, whose job it was to conduct the conclave, moved to the podium, the Chapel quickly fell silent. "In the first ballot for the papacy of the Holy Roman Catholic Church, Cardinal Glouster of France—19 votes, Cardinal Lustini—49 votes, Cardinal Solano—17 votes, Cardinal Zingarni—24 votes, and ten prelates had 1 vote each. This totals 119 votes cast, the number of electors participating in this papal election."

The second ballot was taken immediately. Secretary-of-State Solano knew that this ballot would be about the same, except for the single votes. That would be the interesting thing to watch. Which way would those ten single votes move?

When the Cardinal Chamberlain once again stepped to the rostrum, the conclave quickly came to attention. "Princes of the Church, the results of our second ballot are as follows: Cardinal Glouster of France—21 votes, Cardinal Lustini—55 votes, Cardinal Solano—17 votes, and Cardinal Zingarni—26 votes."

Each cardinal scribbled the vote totals down, slipping the paper into his vestment pocket. These figures would become the subject of midday prayer. They also would serve as the basis for lively discussion and intense negotiations at the lunch table.

"Honorable Princes, please return to conclave at 2 o'clock for your next ballot."

As the cardinals rose to leave, the eyes of Solano locked with those of Cardinal Cassidy of the U.S. The unspoken message passed instantly between them. The United States did not have a viable candidate for the papacy, but the power of the American Church could not be completely ignored, either. The powerful Archbishop of New York did have considerable influence over who would finally be chosen as pope.

Instead of moving toward the dining hall, Cassidy slipped quietly into the private quarters of Solano. Moments later, the Secretary-of-State joined him. Cassidy spoke first. "Your Holiness, if you hold steady, strength for your candidacy may well build."

Solano shook his head. "No. I think we both know that those voting for me merely did so out of loyalty to Paul VII. Furthermore, my age precludes me from being a serious candidate. It looks to me like the die is cast."

"You think the election of Lustini is inevitable?" Cassidy queried.

Solano nodded. "Almost certainly. Those who voted for Glouster would never consider switching to Zingarni with his unorthodox views. Those who favor Zingarni would never be willing to support the hard-line stances of Glouster."

"Yet both of those camps would probably be willing to embrace Lustini," Cassidy interjected.

38

"Exactly," Solano agreed. "Barring some unforeseen development, Cardinal Cassidy, Archbishop Lustini will be the next pope of the Roman Catholic Church."

Solano and Cassidy entered the dining hall together. Every table was engrossed in intense conversation. The suspense hung heavy in the air. Little did the gathering of cardinals know that this conclave was as good as over.

Before the afternoon session began, Solano sent his aide to those electors whom he knew were holding for him. The message was passed. "Solano wishes you to switch your support to Lustini."

With a gentle knock, Solano slipped in the back door of Lustini's living quarters. When Solano entered the sitting room, Lustini greeted him warmly. Solano had hoped that Lustini would be surprised by his visit, but he obviously was not. *This man is way ahead of the game*, Solano noted thoughtfully. *Not many will ever manipulate this pope.*

Solano knew that his planned endorsement would not produce the effect for which he had hoped, now that Lustini already perceived what both he and Cassidy had concluded. But it certainly wouldn't hurt anything, either. "Cardinal Lustini," Solano began, "I believe it is the will of the Holy Spirit that you become the Father of His Church. I have asked those voting for me to switch their allegiance to you. I just wanted you to know my feelings."

Lustini feigned surprise. "But, Cardinal Solano, the conclave is young, and who can tell which way the Spirit's wind may yet blow?" Solano knew full well that Lustini understood the thought processes he had gone through and exactly what his motives were. It was uncanny and considerably unsettling, to say the least, to realize how deep Lustini's insights penetrated!

"No, no," Solano rejoined. "I'm sure your papacy is the will of God, and you have my complete support and devotion."

"Well, thank you, Cardinal. I will never forget this magnificent gesture of kindness. And whatever God's will may be, let's pray that it will be completely accomplished in this conclave," Lustini said warmly.

As the prelates moved toward the Sistine Chapel for the 2 o'clock session, Cardinal Cassidy intercepted Solano in the foyer. "Cardinal Solano, I've been having second thoughts. The course of action that we discussed will result in one of the fastest elections of a pope in the history of the Church. Perhaps we should slow this process down somewhat. If Lustini is swept into the papacy this quickly, his mandate may be perceived as being so strong that we would lose all ability to exercise any influence over him."

Solano's reply came without hesitation. "I've thought that over, Cardinal, but I think there are more important factors that call loudly for a swift conclave with a strong mandate. The global forces presently at work demand that the Church have a strong pope with unquestioned authority. Lustini, whether it be for good or evil, will be a strong pope, and we will present him to the world this afternoon."

When the third vote was taken, the totals came back: Cardinal Glouster of France—23 votes, Cardinal Lustini—74 votes, and Cardinal Zingarni—22 votes. Solano noted mentally that two of his votes had switched to Glouster. He was not surprised. Italy's Cardinal Medino just couldn't bring himself to vote for Lustini, and Poland's Cardinal Minski was committed to a non-Italian pope. It was interesting that four of Zingarni's votes had gone to Lustini this time. The defections had already begun. The prelates were beginning to see the handwriting on the wall.

Secretary-of-State Solano could see the wheels turning in each cardinal's mind. A pope had to be elected by two-thirds. Consequently, 80 votes were needed for an election in this conclave. Lustini stood at 74 votes. It was obvious to every cardinal in the Sistine Chapel which way the wind of the Spirit was blowing.

Not one prelate wished to resist the leading of the Holy Spirit; consequently, each Prince of the Church wrote the name of Cardinal Marlos Lustini on his ballot.

When the Cardinal Chamberlain stepped to the podium for his momentous announcement, the prelates fell silent. "Princes of the Church, the Holy Spirit has expressed His will in a most powerful way. Cardinal Marlos Lustini has been unanimously chosen as the Holy Father of the Holy Roman Catholic Church." Uncharacteristically,

41

the Sistine Chapel was suddenly filled with applause from the Church's princes.

The Cardinal Chamberlain stood in front of Lustini's throne. "Cardinal Marlos Lustini, will you accept the calling to be Father to your Lord's Church and to serve as Vicar of the Son of God?"

With total poise and in just the right tone, Lustini replied, "I accept."

The conclave officer quickly moved from cardinal to cardinal, lowering the canopy over each throne—leaving only Lustini's canopy raised. This action signified the primacy of the position to which Lustini had just been elevated. Now it was time to hear from the new pope.

As Lustini stood to address the conclave, he was a picture of poise and assurance. It seemed obvious to all present that he had been born for this hour.

Lustini began, "My fellow Cardinals, Princes of the Church of Jesus Christ, I am greatly humbled by the action that this conclave has taken today. I am the least of all the servants of Christ; nevertheless, believing in the inerrancy of the working of the Holy Spirit as expressed through you, I do submit myself to that which God's sovereign will has invested in me this day. I would not be truthful if I told you that I was surprised by this divine call. This destiny that I have known I would someday face has been with me for a number of years now."

Glances were exchanged around the room as each cardinal tried to assess how Lustini's unusual disclosure was being received by his fellow prelates. The cardinals leaned forward intently as they sensed that Lustini was about to disclose the name under which he would serve in the papacy. This was always such an important moment because the name that the new pope assumed inevitably provided insight into how he perceived himself and the image that he would portray as the Vicar of the Son of God.

Lustini continued, "Since I was forewarned by the Spirit that this hour would come, I have reflected carefully and prayerfully upon what name I should serve our Lord Jesus and His Church under. Princes of the Church, I believe it is God's will that I be known from this day forward as Pope Peter the Second."

The shock felt by every conclave participant was like a strong jolt of electricity. Pope Peter II! No one had ever dared! Since the man that the Church claimed as its first pope, Pope Peter I, no one had been willing to wear that esteemed name. There had been many to take the name Pope John, Pope Paul, Pope Pius, and even Pope John Paul. But none had ever presumed to assume the name of the original possessor of the keys!

As the cardinals attempted to absorb the implications of the momentous developments that they themselves had helped to unleash, two other pieces of knowledge gnawed at them. The Catholic prophets had foretold that no pope would ever take the name of Peter until the last pope. And it was believed by some that the world would come to an end during the reign of Pope Peter II. Now that reign had begun.

It also was commonly believed in Catholic circles that there was an evil pope coming. Could this Lustini, now Pope Peter II, be that evil pope that many of the faithful had dreaded for so long? What had this conclave unleashed upon the world? Only time would tell...

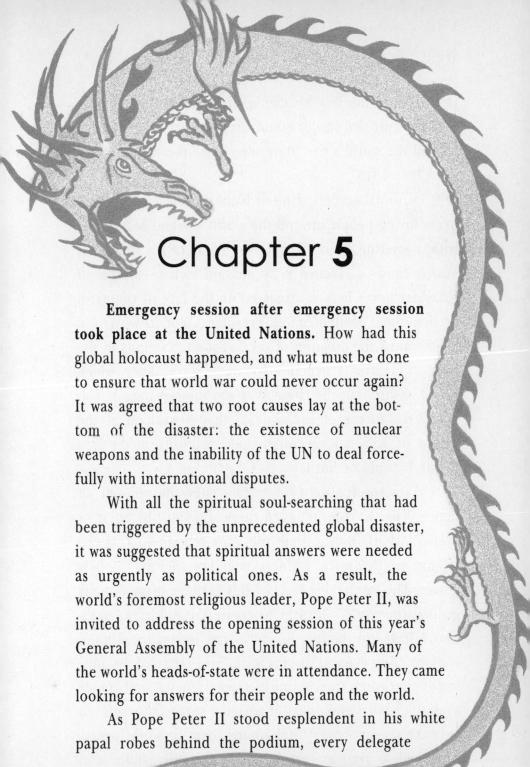

Chapter 5

Emergency session after emergency session took place at the United Nations. How had this global holocaust happened, and what must be done to ensure that world war could never occur again? It was agreed that two root causes lay at the bottom of the disaster: the existence of nuclear weapons and the inability of the UN to deal forcefully with international disputes.

With all the spiritual soul-searching that had been triggered by the unprecedented global disaster, it was suggested that spiritual answers were needed as urgently as political ones. As a result, the world's foremost religious leader, Pope Peter II, was invited to address the opening session of this year's General Assembly of the United Nations. Many of the world's heads-of-state were in attendance. They came looking for answers for their people and the world.

As Pope Peter II stood resplendent in his white papal robes behind the podium, every delegate from each of the 189 member nations hoped against hope that this spiritual leader could supply an answer that had evaded the world's best statesmen since the formation of the UN in 1945.

"National leaders, United Nations delegates, and all peace-loving people around the world, I stand before you with a grieving heart. World War I was called the Great War because it claimed eight million victims—a level of slaughter never before witnessed on the face of the earth at that time. United States President Woodrow Wilson championed the creation of the League of Nations in the hope of creating a structure for world governance, which would ensure that the Great War was the last war. As you know, the forces of isolationism that worshiped at the shrine of national sovereignty aborted this noble idea before it could be born.

"As a result, twenty-two years later the epitome of nationalism, Nazism, plunged the world into the abyss of World War II. By the time the guns fell silent, fifty-two million of the world's finest men lay silently in their graves. The intolerable level of this carnage of war finally goaded the world's leaders to create the noble organization I have the honor of addressing today: the United Nations. But even at its creation, the seeds of its own impotence were treacherously sown into its soul. Once again the shortsightedness of national sovereignty refused to make the necessary total commitment to world peace. The right of veto by certain nations was demanded and given. This effectively tied the UN's right arm behind its back as it was sent forth into a hostile world to attempt to slay the dragon of war and to provide a global home of peace and security.

"Consequently, I stand before you in horror and shock as, even now, we attempt together to bury two billion human beings, one-third of the world's population. Ladies and gentlemen, brothers and sisters, must I point out to you that we no longer have a choice? Is it not obvious to all that we have just received our final warning? We will not have another opportunity to do what we must if we fail our test of courage and resolve at this hour. The time has arrived for national, religious, and personal differences to be set aside in favor of the greater common good. We must now succeed where previous generations have failed. The time has come to fully embrace a structure of international law and to adopt a global leadership that can guide us safely out of the treacherous waters of national conflict and into the safe and secure shores of global cooperation under the benevolent direction of the World Community.

"The last thing that I feel compelled to point out in this, my most urgent appeal ever to the World Community, is the need, not only for world law, but also for world leadership. These goals of which I have spoken today will but fall to the ground unless we have the visionary leadership needed to chart the course that the entire world must now walk. Fortunately, just such visionary leadership is amongst us and willing to assume the responsibilities to which destiny now calls. The only question is—will we follow that leadership, which divine providence has placed on this earth at this strategic time?

"We must act now or there will be no tomorrow! We must now beat our swords into plowshares and our spears into pruning hooks. My dear brothers and sisters, I plead with you! Do not hesitate. Let's banish war forever from the face of this earth. No more war! Never again! Never again!"

The global leaders and the UN delegates sat in awe at the power and the eloquence of the Pontiff's oration. Such clarity of vision and force of logic had seldom, if ever, been brought to bear on this august world forum. As the Pope turned from the podium, the entire General Assembly rose to its feet as one man in thunderous applause. Tears glistened in the eyes of the world's leaders, and a new resolution surged through the hearts of each person present. "We will not fail! We will not be deterred! We will have courage and build a genuine world order—free of war, free of fear."

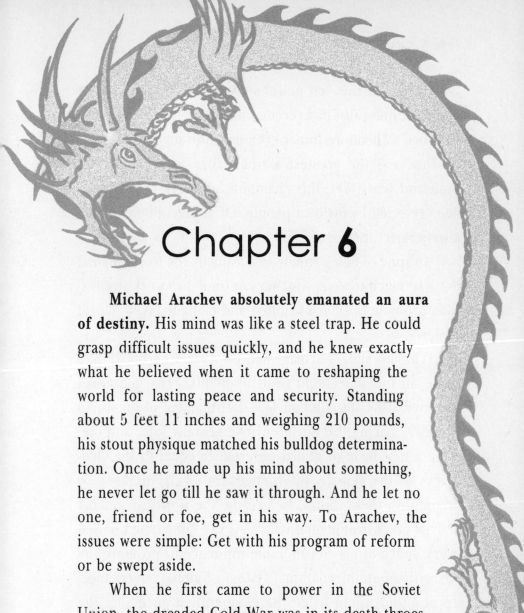

Chapter 6

Michael Arachev absolutely emanated an aura of destiny. His mind was like a steel trap. He could grasp difficult issues quickly, and he knew exactly what he believed when it came to reshaping the world for lasting peace and security. Standing about 5 feet 11 inches and weighing 210 pounds, his stout physique matched his bulldog determination. Once he made up his mind about something, he never let go till he saw it through. And he let no one, friend or foe, get in his way. To Arachev, the issues were simple: Get with his program of reform or be swept aside.

When he first came to power in the Soviet Union, the dreaded Cold War was in its death throes. People around the world watched in amazement as the barbed wire of the Iron Curtain was rolled up. Not one person on the earth would ever forget the feeling of relief and hope that swelled up when young East Germans started streaming over the top of the hated Berlin Wall.

When Arachev left power six years later, the threat of a nuclear holocaust had receded dramatically. World News Network's Theodore Joiner even dared to say that Michael Arachev was the greatest world leader in the past two thousand years! Yet, this champion of peace had actually been rejected by his own people. Of course, don't people always reject their messiahs?

In spite of being rudely cast aside by the world he had done so much to save, Arachev continued to work tirelessly to promote his much vaunted and maligned New World Order.

The horrible nuclear meltdown at Chernobyl had made an indelible impression upon him. His goals had included achieving total nuclear disarmament of the world by 1999, making the world environmentally safe, and creating a new form of global governance equal to the challenges of the globally interdependent electronic age. To accomplish these things, he became the world's foremost activist on environmental issues. At the same time he used every ounce of his considerable influence to promote the necessity of an international system of global governance. To any who would listen, he eloquently argued that the day of the nation-state was over and the time for international government had arrived. Arachev also quietly organized worldwide meetings of those behind-the-scenes "king-makers" whom he knew had the power and the influence to bring a world governmental system into being. These meetings commonly featured speeches from high-profile former military generals. These speeches passionately implored the world to save itself from total annihilation by enacting nuclear disarmament for the entire globe.

All of the world's leaders knew that Arachev had lobbied tirelessly for a nuclear-free world by 1999. Now they were painfully aware of the fact that, had they listened, this horrific tragedy would not have occurred. At Arachev's yearly forums, the world's best minds had attempted to map the path to world peace. But one obstacle always remained stubbornly in the way: national sovereignty. They all knew what to do, but powerful nations—the United States in particular—refused to surrender their veto power so that the United Nations could become a bona fide world government. It now seemed apparent to all that the time had come to turn to this extraordinary leader who had brought the Cold War to an end, but who had been prevented from leading the world on into the promised land of the New World Order.

In the wake of the nuclear disaster, Michael Arachev seemed to be everywhere—making speeches, expressing condolences, supplying answers. It seemed that here was a man whose time had genuinely come. He had not been idle all those years while out of political power; he had been working diligently on a plan for global governance for a time that he was sure would someday come. That time had arrived. And the world had never been more ready for a strong man with answers!

Massive teams of doctors were recruited from all over the world to ease the suffering of those dying from nuclear fallout and to help those who could be saved. All the nations of the world donated millions of dollars in supplies, equipment, and manpower to bury the dead throughout Asia. In the meantime, the United States struggled to deal with twenty million dead and dying as a result of China's final revenge.

On the global scene, actions previously unthinkable were accepted without question. Nations began wholesale disarmament and declared NATO to be a world police force under UN authority. Russia and many other nations joined this retooled, world peacekeeping body. It was appropriately renamed World Alliance for Peace and Safety (WAPS).

International disputes previously allowed to fester were now settled boldly and resolutely by UN resolutions. One by one, the world's trouble spots were dealt with—Bosnia, Chechnya, and even Northern Ireland. Only the Gordian knot of the Middle East remained an issue.

But, Michael Arachev had made up his mind that he would suffer no opposition. The days of war and conflict were over—period. The world's nations would bow to the authority of international law—or else. He had once before made the mistake of being too weak and indecisive. He would not let it happen again.

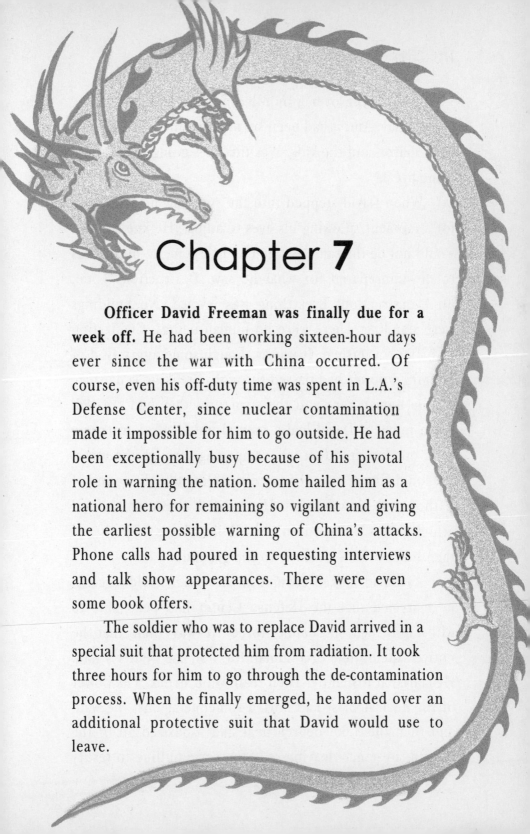

Chapter 7

Officer David Freeman was finally due for a week off. He had been working sixteen-hour days ever since the war with China occurred. Of course, even his off-duty time was spent in L.A.'s Defense Center, since nuclear contamination made it impossible for him to go outside. He had been exceptionally busy because of his pivotal role in warning the nation. Some hailed him as a national hero for remaining so vigilant and giving the earliest possible warning of China's attacks. Phone calls had poured in requesting interviews and talk show appearances. There were even some book offers.

The soldier who was to replace David arrived in a special suit that protected him from radiation. It took three hours for him to go through the de-contamination process. When he finally emerged, he handed over an additional protective suit that David would use to leave.

It had been over a month since David had seen the light of day. And it had been six months since he had been with Sharon and the kids. Was this ever going to be a welcome break!

When David stepped into the sunlight, he stood still for a moment, allowing his eyes to adjust. He knew things would not be the same as when he had gone in, but he was totally unprepared for what he saw. Destruction! Total, utter destruction! Everything was leveled. No buildings were standing. There were no human beings. Civilization had simply vanished. It was as though some angry God of unlimited power had passed through, wreaking vengeance on the human race and the structures they had created. For a moment David had a mental vision of an awesome God, one hundred feet tall, rampaging through the earth. He could almost hear His voice rumbling like the sound of a thousand thunders as He twisted the architectural achievements of men into pretzel-like pieces of junk and then hurled them violently to the ground!

As David looked around at this other-worldly scene, he marveled that the Defense Center had been able to withstand such incredible force. It was then that he noticed the outline of a human form on the Center's wall. He stared at it silently. Then realization struck. The power of the nuclear blast had hurled someone against the wall, and then the 3,000-degree heat had vaporized all of the human substance, leaving only the eerie outline to testify

54

that this poor person had ever existed. The remains resembled a charcoal rendering of a life now forgotten.

David's knees suddenly turned to jelly, and fear encased itself around his heart. His hands shook uncontrollably. Never had he experienced the awareness of the reality of God as he did right then. If this was God in His fury, then David never wanted to be the target of that wrath!

By sheer force of will, David snapped himself back to reality. Only the nuclear-free vehicle that was waiting to take him to the de-contamination center gave any indication that anything living remained on earth.

As they traveled north, away from L.A., the extent of the devastation began to decrease, little by little. Metal beams that once supported large buildings still stood, even though they had twisted into grotesque shapes under the intense heat of the nuclear explosion. David was astounded as he tried to imagine the force that could twist four-foot-wide metal beams as though they were made of rubber! As they continued farther, a few scattered buildings remained standing. But there were still no human beings in evidence.

About 50 miles north of Los Angeles, David saw the big sign, "End of Lethal Radiation Zone." Immediately, they began to meet cars. A few people appeared on the sidewalks in the towns through which they traveled. Twenty miles farther, things really started to appear normal.

Upon his arrival at the de-contamination center, David was immediately directed to a shower designed to remove as much radiation as possible from his protective suit. He then was guided to the next specially designed room for the removal of the anti-radiation suit. Over the speaker system, an emotionless voice instructed him to pass as quickly as possible through the heavy lead doors to his left the instant he was able to extricate himself from his anti-radiation coveralls.

Once past the double lead doors, David was escorted to a special shower using special chemicals. After he emerged from that shower, he moved to a normal shower for rinsing. As he finally slipped into the fresh clean uniform that had been brought for him, he breathed a sigh of relief. *Am I ever glad that is over*, he thought.

Leaving the de-contamination center, he resumed his trip north toward San Francisco. David's flight left from there. Normally his scheduled flight would have stopped through Denver, but of course, Denver was no more. All planes now stopped through Las Vegas on their trips to the east.

When his flight finally touched down in Cincinnati, Ohio, David's pulse quickened. He knew that Sharon, David Jr., and Misty would be waiting for him. It had been too long!

David's family ran over to him the minute he stepped through the gates. David Jr. grabbed him first. Then he felt Misty's little arms wrap around his leg. He picked her up and squeezed her tight as he tousled David's hair with his other hand. After a minute or two, he turned his attention to Sharon. When he looked into her eyes, big tears slid down her face, and she melted into his arms. "I didn't know if I would ever see you again," she murmured as she clung tightly to him.

"I know exactly how you feel. I wondered myself. Oh, Sharon, I didn't realize how much you meant to me. I don't ever want to leave you again." The words just came pouring out of David. There was so much that he needed to say that he had neglected to say before. He would not make that mistake ever again. He had determined on the flight home that from now on he would say what he felt. A man never knows when it might be his last chance!

During the short week he was home, David listened continually to the news reports. The entire United States was on an emergency footing while attempting to deal with the aftermath of China's attack.

All areas within a fifty-mile radius of each of the nuclear explosions were declared off limits. Wherever the nuclear rains had fallen, the crops in the fields had to be destroyed and properly disposed of. Millions of cows, chickens, and other animals that were affected by the radiation needed to be buried. The manpower required to deal with this unprecedented situation was absolutely overwhelming.

In the aftermath, America's stock market plunged downward until it lost two-thirds of its value. Major companies had sustained massive property losses, not to mention the loss of key personnel. It would require many years to rebuild. As a result, economic leadership swung like a huge pendulum to the European Union. America's preeminence in world affairs was temporarily ended, if not forever.

Not all results of America's catastrophe were negative. Those who lived through the holocaust had a new appreciation for life. Community spirit was rediscovered. People worked side by side to rebuild the nation. Most importantly, a great spiritual revival began to sweep across the land. Churches were filled to capacity. Midweek Bible study groups were commonplace in every community. The Ten Commandments suddenly reappeared in schools, government buildings, and other public places— and no one raised a voice of objection. It was as though a malignant tumor had been surgically removed from the American soul.

During his week at home, David himself dealt with the spiritual question. On Wednesday, Sharon suggested that they attend church that evening. Before the attack, David would never have considered it, and he wasn't sure that Sharon would have asked. Now, however, it seemed that almost everyone was undergoing significant changes in their previously held values.

Sharon especially wanted to go to this particular meeting because the speaker's subject was titled, "The Chinese-American War in Bible Prophecy." When David heard that, he knew he definitely did not want to miss it.

That evening, they entered a packed sanctuary and found a seat in the back. They watched with interest as Roger Cornell, the prophecy teacher for the meeting, opened his lecture by reading the Bible passage containing the prophecy:

> *And the four angels were loosed, which were prepared for an hour, and a day, and a month, and a year, for to slay the third part of men. And the number of the army of the horsemen were two hundred thousand thousand: and I heard the number of them.* Revelation 9:15-16

David saw immediately where the teacher was going. This 2,000-year-old prophecy foretold a war that would kill one-third part of men. The world had just experienced a war that had, in fact, killed one-third of the world's population! David couldn't believe it!

He listened intently as Roger Cornell explained that Mao Tse Tung, an earlier leader of China, had actually boasted in his diary that he could field an army of 200 million soldiers. That was the exact number of the army that was prophesied to start this war. Wow! David had never heard anything like this before. He continued to focus his attention on the prophecy teacher.

Cornell went on to say that the Chinese-American conflict was only one of the major prophecies of the Bible. He explained that a world government would arise to power out of all this chaos. There would be some kind of a covenant confirmed in the Middle East that would pave the way for Israel to build her Third Temple.

What I want to know, David thought, *is what all this means, and where does it lead?* He didn't have to wait long to get his answer.

Cornell continued, "Things are going to get worse before they get better. The forces that have long dreamed of one-world government will use this horrible calamity to usher in their vision. Anyone who resists their plan for this New World Order will be considered an extremist and an enemy of peace. This will ultimately degenerate into political and economic persecution of all who do not agree with this new global structure."

This guy makes so much sense! David agreed. *But I still want to know where all this ends up.*

Cornell continued to speak. "Shortly after Israel builds her Third Temple, a time of Great Tribulation will begin. This Great Tribulation will last for three and one-half years. People will be forced to pledge allegiance to the New World Order and its leader, a man the Bible calls the antichrist. Anyone who refuses to pledge allegiance to the antichrist and his one-world system will be forbidden access to the economy. The Book of Revelation, chapter 13, tells us that they will not be permitted to buy or sell."

"So that's how the 'mark of the beast' that I've heard about all of my life will work," David commented to himself.

"After the three and one-half years of Great Tribulation, the World Community will decide to invade Israel to settle the status of Jerusalem, once and for all," Cornell explained. "This will result in the Battle of Armageddon. I'm sure all of you have heard of that battle." The audience listened soberly.

As David and Sharon drove home that night, they discussed all the things that Roger Cornell had taught. "David, what do you think of what he said?" Sharon finally asked.

"The prophecy about the war that would kill one-third of the human race blew me away!" David answered. "I couldn't believe that was in the Bible!"

"You know, David, experiencing this war and then hearing this prophecy lecture tonight is causing me to rethink my priorities," Sharon stated soberly.

"I know exactly how you feel," David agreed. "We've got some changes to make in our lives, don't we?" He squeezed Sharon's hand tightly. David had never felt so right about the direction in which their lives were headed as he did right now.

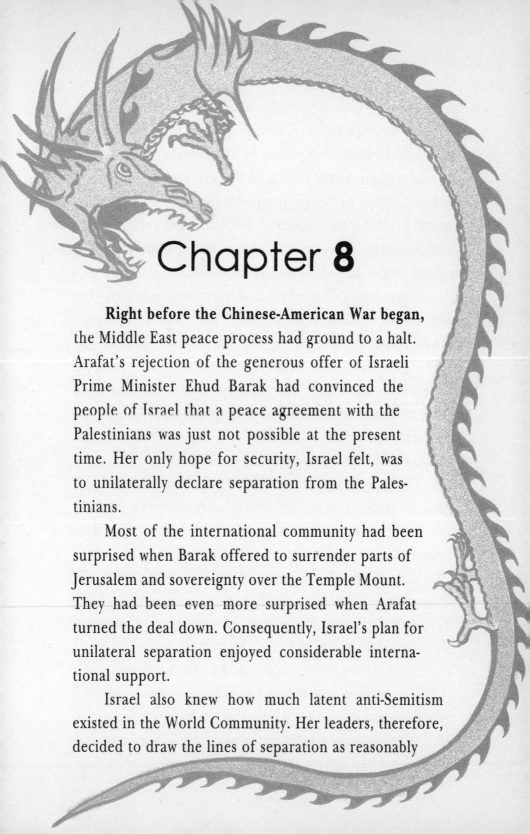

Chapter **8**

Right before the Chinese-American War began, the Middle East peace process had ground to a halt. Arafat's rejection of the generous offer of Israeli Prime Minister Ehud Barak had convinced the people of Israel that a peace agreement with the Palestinians was just not possible at the present time. Her only hope for security, Israel felt, was to unilaterally declare separation from the Palestinians.

Most of the international community had been surprised when Barak offered to surrender parts of Jerusalem and sovereignty over the Temple Mount. They had been even more surprised when Arafat turned the deal down. Consequently, Israel's plan for unilateral separation enjoyed considerable international support.

Israel also knew how much latent anti-Semitism existed in the World Community. Her leaders, therefore, decided to draw the lines of separation as reasonably as possible. Furthermore, Israel secretly consulted with Michael Arachev concerning the fairness of her plan. The Israelis held Michael Arachev in high regard since he had helped seven hundred thousand Russian Jews to immigrate to Israel. They had even given him their most prestigious peace prize for his actions. To their delight, Arachev diplomatically conveyed the impression that he would be willing to give the plan his tacit approval.

When Israel's leaders made the announcement that they would impose separation between the Palestinians and Israelis, the outcry from the Arab world was loud and predictable. However, Israel, for the most part, modeled her solution after the "almost" agreement that had been negotiated at Camp David back in July of 2000. This was the agreement that most of the World Community felt Arafat should have accepted.

The Palestinians would have their state, of course. It was only right. Most of the territories captured by Israel in the 1967 Six-Day War would be returned to Palestinian control. Israeli settlers living in those territories that were returned would be compensated financially if they chose to resettle in Israel proper. If they chose to remain in the West Bank, they would submit themselves to Palestinian government and laws.

The Palestinians' capital would be in the small suburb of East Jerusalem called Abu Dis. They accepted this solution temporarily, while at the same time protesting that there would never be total peace until all of East Jerusalem was returned to Arab control.

Israel would retain control of the Temple Mount, while allowing the two Muslim holy places located there to be administered by Muslim clerics. Israel's unilateral separation plan even provided for a corridor connecting Palestinian-controlled territory to the two mosques. This eliminated the continual friction generated by the border checks that Palestinians despised so much.

Then came the astounding announcement: Israel would build her long-desired Third Temple. It would be built in the open area north of the Dome of the Rock. The right-wing faction in Israel railed against the agreement that left the two "pagan shrines" on the Temple Mount, but the liberals convinced the people that the time for a solution, imposed as it was, had finally arrived. Besides this, the word that Arachev had given the plan his stamp of approval led Israelis to believe that this solution would enjoy the support of the international community.

Even while the conservatives tried to marshal opposition to the separation plan, the lure of building the Third Temple after two thousand years seemed to take all the steam out of their resistance. The Israeli government knew that without the U.S. veto, which had recently been abolished, Israel had no choice but to take what she could get. Arachev's support for the plan was key.

It did not take long for the Mideast separation plan to be implemented. The only problems encountered came from the West Bank settlers who didn't want to leave their settlements. But they didn't want to live under Palestinian authority, either. When they protested that God had promised this land to their father Abraham, Arachev rebuked them in no uncertain terms. "That kind of thinking has gotten you nothing but war for the past one hundred years. The time has come for peace." Many of the Israelis were actually glad to see someone put the settlers in their place. They had stood in the way of a solution for too long already.

Following the plan's implementation, a time of peace and safety descended over the land of Israel. There were no bombings, no shelling from the north, not even any stone throwing. The Palestinians were busy establishing their capital in Abu Dis, and Israel was moving into high gear to construct its temple. Enthusiasm was so high that it was hard to complain about anything.

Most people agreed on one thing, even if they could not agree on anything else: Michael Arachev was supplying the leadership that this world had needed for a long, long time.

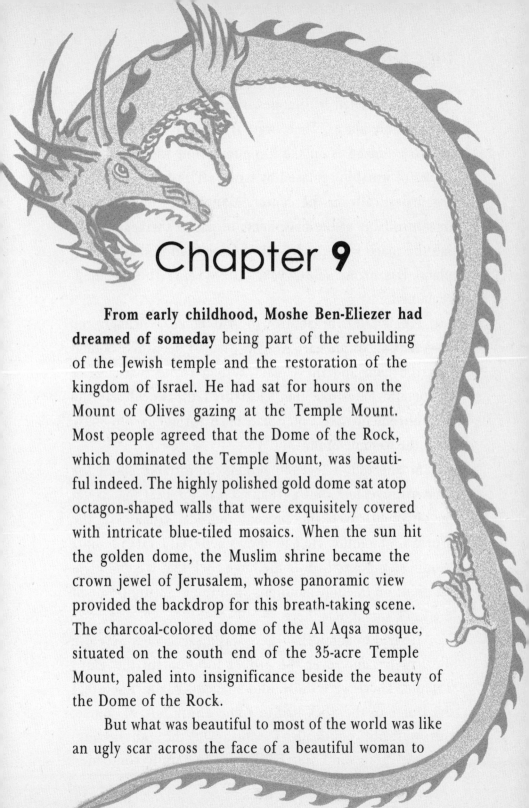

Chapter **9**

**From early childhood, Moshe Ben-Eliezer had
dreamed of someday** being part of the rebuilding
of the Jewish temple and the restoration of the
kingdom of Israel. He had sat for hours on the
Mount of Olives gazing at the Temple Mount.
Most people agreed that the Dome of the Rock,
which dominated the Temple Mount, was beautiful indeed. The highly polished gold dome sat atop
octagon-shaped walls that were exquisitely covered
with intricate blue-tiled mosaics. When the sun hit
the golden dome, the Muslim shrine became the
crown jewel of Jerusalem, whose panoramic view
provided the backdrop for this breath-taking scene.
The charcoal-colored dome of the Al Aqsa mosque,
situated on the south end of the 35-acre Temple
Mount, paled into insignificance beside the beauty of
the Dome of the Rock.

But what was beautiful to most of the world was like
an ugly scar across the face of a beautiful woman to

Moshe. He boiled with anger when he looked at the two Muslim holy places. There were days when he would close his eyes and envision the Temple Mount with the pagan places of worship replaced by Israel's Third Temple standing majestically in the center. Many times he had wept uncontrollably at the blasphemy of pagan shrines occupying the place where the God of Israel had said He would place His name. But, year after year, the problem remained.

Finally, the breakthrough had come. Through the intervention of Michael Arachev, it had been determined that the land and the Holy City had to be shared. The diplomatic milestone that electrified the world was the announcement that a plan had been formulated to share even the Temple Mount.

Moshe didn't feel altogether comfortable about the final arrangement, but perhaps it was the best that could be obtained given the present political climate in the World Community. He had always believed Israel's temple should stand exactly over the huge rock that was the highest point on the holy mountain. But the beautiful Dome of the Rock shrine was there.

He had to admit that there was disagreement, even in the Israeli camp, over the proper location for the Third Temple. There were those who adamantly contended that the Dome of the Rock had to come down; but, of course, this was not politically feasible. On the other hand, Hebrew Professor Yosef Eddlestein forcefully contended that the First and Second Temples were built to the north of the Dome of the Rock and that the Holy of Holies was located exactly where the small cupola marked the Dome of the Spirits. The professor never tired of explaining that building the Third Temple just north of the Dome of the Rock would leave the Dome of the Rock in the area known in the Bible as the Outer Court or the Court of the Gentiles. Eddlestein argued that, since this area was known as the Court of the Gentiles, it would be possible to leave the gold-domed Arab shrine undisturbed, allowing the Muslims to continue worshiping there.

In his heart Moshe had always felt that the temple should replace the Dome. However, he had to admit that no one knew for certain where the original temple site was. Some said this, and some said that. Perhaps it was enough that the temple was going to be built after two thousand years of nonexistence. Still, the thought of the two pagan shrines remaining permanently on the Temple Mount filled him with revulsion. He sighed. Ultimately, it was in God's hands.

Shoving all of these conflicting emotions aside, Moshe returned to the reality at hand. After all, this was a great moment! For two thousand years the Jewish people had been without a homeland. For two thousand years, Israel had worshiped without a temple. But just in his lifetime, the nation had been reborn and Jerusalem recaptured.

And now, to think that the time had come to place the cornerstone that would launch the construction of the

Third Temple! What more could he want? On the spot, Moshe decided to place his trust in God concerning all the things he did not understand and to relish the historic events that he himself was privileged to participate in.

Several years earlier, Moshe had personally roamed the Negev Desert in southern Israel for days, along with his friend Omri, looking for the perfect stone that would serve as the cornerstone of the Third Temple. The rugged terrain was literally filled with stones of all shapes and sizes. But not just any stone would do. This stone was to serve as the focal point for construction of Israel's first temple in two thousand years!

Early one Tuesday morning, they came upon a great rock slide. There in the midst of the rubble lay a beautiful, solid marble stone that was just perfect for the beginning of God's house. The white stone was five feet long, two and a half feet wide and deep, and weighed approximately four thousand pounds.

Moshe flipped open his cell phone and called the wrecker service with whom he had made previous arrangements—just in case his search was successful. When the wrecker arrived, cables were slid under the new cornerstone by digging grooves in the sand. Once the cables were securely fastened, the wrecker's wench slowly hoisted the stone into the air. Moshe beamed with satisfaction as the stone was then lowered onto the bed of the truck that he had rented. Then, riding with the wrecker's operator, Omri and Moshe headed for Jerusalem.

Moshe and Omri decided it was time to take a huge leap of faith. They would actually begin the construction of the Third Temple by placing the cornerstone on the Temple Mount. God would have to do the rest. It seemed like a totally unrealistic act to the skeptics. But wasn't the God of Israel a God of miracles? The books of the prophets were replete with miraculous accounts of little steps of faith resulting in great victories for the nation of Israel. God could do it again!

As the truck slowly made its way through the streets of Jerusalem, the huge stone attracted curious glances from passers-by. When Moshe saw Rahman Husseini's long, hard stare, he knew there would be trouble. Husseini had been the leader of the Arab opposition to any Jewish presence or activity whatsoever on the Temple Mount. Moshe was almost sure Husseini had recognized him riding in the passenger seat of the truck. "We'd better hurry," Moshe said to his driver.

Sympathizers to their cause had already paved the way for access to the Temple Mount area. As they approached the final ascent to the Mount itself, Moshe noticed a gathering crowd. Leading the crowd was Rahman Husseini. Moshe frowned. Just then the mob closed, blocking further progress. The truck ground to a halt, the cornerstone still strapped in place. Within minutes, arguments and shoving broke out as Jewish sympathizers attempted to clear the way for Moshe and his cornerstone. Moshe knew this scene could turn ugly real quick, but he had total faith that God was with them.

Others were not so sure. Realizing there was going to be trouble, someone called the police. When the forces arrived, stones began to be hurled this way and that. Soon, total chaos had erupted.

By the time order was finally restored, 17 Arabs were dead and many Arabs and Jews wounded. The bloody scene occupied the front pages of newspapers around the world, and debate concerning Israel's handling of the riot dominated the proceedings in the halls of the United Nations.

As a result of all the trouble he had caused, Moshe Ben-Eliezer was banned from setting foot on the Temple Mount. So he placed his cornerstone just outside the Temple Mount wall in anticipation of the day it could be installed and temple construction begun.

Now that day was just around the corner!

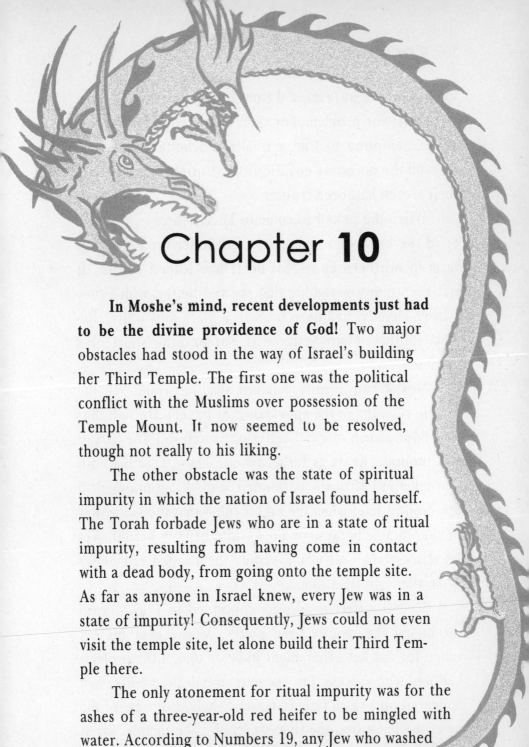

Chapter 10

In Moshe's mind, recent developments just had to be the divine providence of God! Two major obstacles had stood in the way of Israel's building her Third Temple. The first one was the political conflict with the Muslims over possession of the Temple Mount. It now seemed to be resolved, though not really to his liking.

The other obstacle was the state of spiritual impurity in which the nation of Israel found herself. The Torah forbade Jews who are in a state of ritual impurity, resulting from having come in contact with a dead body, from going onto the temple site. As far as anyone in Israel knew, every Jew was in a state of impurity! Consequently, Jews could not even visit the temple site, let alone build their Third Temple there.

The only atonement for ritual impurity was for the ashes of a three-year-old red heifer to be mingled with water. According to Numbers 19, any Jew who washed in this mixture was cleansed from being spiritually impure. Herein lay the problem. For many years religious Jews had been attempting to find a totally red heifer that could meet all the necessary qualifications. Until three years ago, their search had been fruitless.

When the news had come to Moshe three years earlier of the birth of a completely red heifer on a religious farm in northern Israel, his heart had leaped for joy. It was even more incredible that the red heifer, which they named Melody, had been born to a black and white Holstein mother. Many believed it was nothing short of a miracle!

Moshe had already believed that he would see the temple rebuilt and the appearance of Israel's Messiah. But the sudden birth of a red heifer on Israeli soil, the first in two thousand years as far as anyone knew, sent his faith skyrocketing! Moshe was flooded with disappointment a few months later when the rabbis ruled that the heifer was not acceptable because of a few white hairs in her tail. Yet he was certain God would supply the needed red heifer when the right time came.

Several different projects continued to work toward producing the required red heifer. Moshe kept his ear tuned for any news that might indicate one of the projects had met with success. Just recently, the desired heifer had appeared on a small farm in Israel. When Moshe heard the news, he knew that the time to rebuild the temple was at hand. Just the thought of the momentous events ahead sent Moshe's heart rejoicing! This time news concerning the heifer was kept quiet, since all the publicity surrounding Melody had only led to disappointment and, from some quarters, ridicule.

It was amazing that the same year the heifer turned three years of age, Israel's separation plan cleared the way for the building of the Third Temple. Could this be coincidence? Moshe didn't think so.

The day for the offering of the red heifer had arrived, and Moshe was filled with anticipation. It would be the first legitimate offering of a sacrifice for Israel since the destruction of the Second Temple in 70 A.D.! He arrived early at the Mount of Olives, where the red heifer was to be killed. The sacred mount was already teeming with rabbis in their black garments and with ordinary Israelis who had turned out to witness this genuinely historic occasion.

People were standing in groups, talking animatedly concerning the ancient act they were about to witness. "Will this trigger the appearance of our Messiah?" one asked. "Could He even manifest Himself today?"

"I don't think Messiah will appear until after the temple is completed," another speculated. And so the conversations went.

Moshe rolled all of these things over in his mind as he walked along. He had always believed that Messiah would appear once the Third Temple was completed. That was the reason he had been so driven to do his part in the construction of the temple. He couldn't wait to see how it all played out!

At the appointed time, the procession began in the Kidron Valley at the bottom of the Mount of Olives. Moshe and everyone else jockeyed for position in order to obtain a better view of the ceremony. As the attending priests made their way slowly up the hill, the musical instruments played and the Levites sang. All the participants had been carefully trained to carry out their particular responsibilities. The red heifer was led along behind by two strong young priests. Moshe could barely contain his tears. It was certainly a defining moment in Israel's history!

The revered 12th Century Jewish teacher Maimonides had stated that, during the time of Israel's tenth red heifer, the Messiah would be revealed. There had been nine red heifers in Israel's history until now. Today's would be the tenth. Most of those present had no doubt that they were witnessing the ushering in of the messianic era!

Upon reaching the top of the Mount of Olives, the attending priests formed two lines, creating a pathway leading up to the place of sacrifice that had been chosen.

Just in front of the red heifer walked Israel's two chief rabbis.

When all was in place, Chief Rabbi Cohen, recently named High Priest Cohen, stepped forward to pray. A silent hush descended upon the crowd. "Lord God, blessed be Your name. We thank You for providing at this time the required sacrifice for the cleansing of Your people from spiritual uncleanness. Lord, You have brought us from the north, the south, the east, and the west as You promised, and You have placed us in this land, this Holy Land. For this we praise You. Now, Lord, accept this sacrifice and use it for the full redemption of Your people to Yourself and for the construction of Your house, Your temple, where You promised our father David that You would place Your name. Amen."

Moshe looked down over the city of Jerusalem, tears in his eyes. What a beautiful and breathtaking sight it was! There was no scene in the entire world that could compare to Jerusalem from the Mount of Olives. In the foreground, on the slopes of the Mount, were thousands of graves. Those buried there believed that they would be the first to rise from the dead at the prophesied coming of the Messiah to the Mount of Olives.

Then, just across the Kidron Valley, were the majestic walls of the Temple Mount and the Old City of Jerusalem. Immediately between Moshe and the place where the new temple would stand was the sealed Eastern Gate with all the mystery that surrounded it. Jews and Christians alike believed that the Messiah would enter through that gate when He came. Knowing that the Jews believed this, the Turkish leader Suleiman the Magnificent, in 1517, had his masons seal the gate shut in an attempt to ensure that the Messiah would not enter there. Little did he know that he had inadvertently fulfilled the prophecy of Ezekiel 44, which stated that the gate would be shut because the Messiah had entered in by it, and that it would remain shut until Messiah entered through it the second time.

In the 1967 War, when Israel was planning its attack on the Old City of Jerusalem, one of the soldiers suggested surprising the Arabs by blasting the Eastern Gate open and entering that way. The commander vetoed that plan, stating flatly that the Eastern Gate was to be opened only when the Messiah came.

Moshe's eyes scanned the beautiful city of Jerusalem behind and to the north of the Temple Mount. Churches, mosques, hotels, homes, and business all seemed to be nestled around the Temple Mount—the center of the city and of the world. And now, the house of God would again be built on the hill where God had chosen to place His name!

He tried to visualize what the Temple Mount would look like once the Third Temple was completed. The Dome of the Rock and the Al Aqsa Mosque stood imposingly on the Temple Mount, ruining his mental vision. *It's just not going to be right with them there*, he thought. *Maybe*

*God will supernaturally move them before the beginning of con-
struction next week.*

The priests were now positioning the heifer to face
toward the temple site, as they had been instructed. When
everything was prepared, the appointed Levite stepped
forward in his priestly garments, which the Temple Institute had carefully designed according to the Mosaic
instructions. Moshe thought, *It's a good thing the Temple
Institute, by faith, recreated all of these things in advance, or
else we wouldn't have been prepared for this momentous time.*

The knife swept downward swiftly into the neck of
the young heifer, cleanly severing the jugular vein. She
quivered, jerked violently, then dropped to the ground.
The younger priests dragged her onto the altar where she
was to be burnt and where the precious ashes would be
carefully collected and placed in the proper container.

Once the burning was over and the ashes collected,
High Priest Cohen made the important announcement.
"Tomorrow the process of purification will begin. All
those who are involved in the construction of the Third
Temple will go first. As you know, the purification process
takes seven days."

Early the next morning, Moshe was near the front of
the line for the purification ceremony. He watched as the
priests took a small amount of the ashes from yesterday's
sacrifice and mixed it into quite a large amount of water.
Then the announcement came: "All of you to be purified
must not have come into contact with a dead body in any

way for the past three days. If you have contacted a dead body, including visiting a cemetery, you must wait until three days have expired."

Moshe thought carefully. *When was the last funeral I attended? Have I been too close to a cemetery? No. I think I'm all right.*

When his time came, the priest smiled. "Is that cornerstone ready to go, Moshe?"

"It certainly is. We've already arranged for the crane to move it and set it in place," Moshe replied happily.

"Praise be unto God!" the priest exulted.

Moshe washed himself carefully in the sacred mixture. He couldn't really say that he felt any different after the ceremony, but he certainly started watching where he went after that. He wouldn't be able to visit his father's grave from now on—unless he wanted to go through the purification process all over again. He wouldn't be able to take that shortcut through the cemetery on the way home from prayer at the Western Wall anymore. And if he visited friends in the hospital, he'd have to make sure that no dead bodies were nearby. Hmm...this was going to be a little tricky.

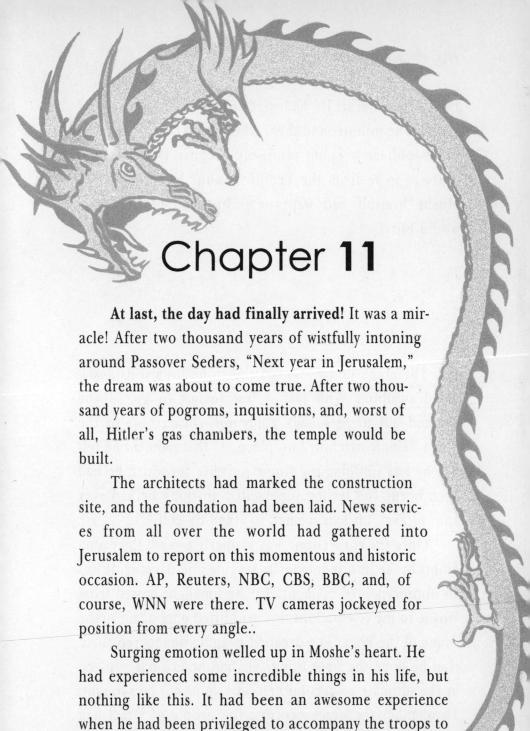

Chapter 11

At last, the day had finally arrived! It was a miracle! After two thousand years of wistfully intoning around Passover Seders, "Next year in Jerusalem," the dream was about to come true. After two thousand years of pogroms, inquisitions, and, worst of all, Hitler's gas chambers, the temple would be built.

The architects had marked the construction site, and the foundation had been laid. News services from all over the world had gathered into Jerusalem to report on this momentous and historic occasion. AP, Reuters, NBC, CBS, BBC, and, of course, WNN were there. TV cameras jockeyed for position from every angle..

Surging emotion welled up in Moshe's heart. He had experienced some incredible things in his life, but nothing like this. It had been an awesome experience when he had been privileged to accompany the troops to the Temple Mount at the time of its capture in the

1967 Six-Day War. He had watched soldiers fighting and killing one minute, and then, when the Arabs fled, those same soldiers weeping profusely because two thousand years of exile from the Temple Mount had just ended. Moshe himself had wept until he thought his heart would burst.

The crane slowly lowered the stone toward its designated position. With just a few inches to go, Moshe reached out to personally guide the cornerstone of the Third Temple carefully into place. At that moment he felt like he was fulfilling the single purpose for which he had been born. The feeling superseded anything he had ever known! Even his hair seemed to stand on end.

Once the cornerstone was properly placed, the young rabbis broke into spontaneous singing and dancing. It was an unprecedented moment. As the limelight passed from Moshe to the celebrations, his eyes lifted once again to the Dome of the Rock. The dreaded nagging doubts returned. Had he done the right thing? Or had he just participated in the ultimate compromise? *God help us all*, he thought. Throughout the peace process, the people of Israel had gotten used to the art of compromise. Had it finally gotten to him as well? Instead of the exhilaration that he knew he should be experiencing, Moshe returned home that evening with a sick feeling in the pit of his stomach.

The construction of the Third Temple moved very rapidly. The huge cranes that had been erected just outside the Temple Mount walls swung back and forth constantly, lifting the large amount of stone needed for the construction onto the building site.

Herod's Second Temple had been a huge structure. Some historians stated that it was 17 stories high. Such a building would have dwarfed the Dome of the Rock and would not really have been in keeping with the spirit of sharing the Temple Mount. Besides, there wasn't enough room for that size of structure in the area north of the Dome of the Rock.

The decision was made to design the Third Temple according to the dimensions of Solomon's First Temple. The Scriptures described Solomon's Temple itself as being 90 feet long, 30 feet wide, and 45 feet high. Added to this were the ornate walls surrounding the outer court, together with a number of large porticoes.

The finest white marble available on the face of the earth was chosen for the temple's exterior. The quality of the marble was so exquisite that it almost took on the appearance of translucent alabaster. Moshe had never seen anything quite like it.

The Temple's windows were tall and narrow, accentuating the height of the Temple. The stained glass windows were created to portray the history of the nation of Israel. The first window depicted Abraham on Mount Moriah with his knife raised over his son Isaac. After that was Jacob wrestling with the angel the night his name was changed to Israel. Then came Moses with the Ten Commandments in his hands. Many other pivotal historic scenes followed: Samson killing one thousand Philistines with the jawbone of an ass; Elijah confronting the prophets of Baal; David killing Goliath with a sling; Ezekiel prophesying to the valley of dry bones; the Nazi holocaust; and the rebirth of Israel in 1948. The last scene was of Shlomo Goren sounding the blast on the shofar at the Wailing Wall when Jerusalem was reunited in the 1967 War.

The finest builders in the world were enlisted to build the Third Temple. The result was the most stunningly beautiful building on the face of the earth.

Moshe Ben-Eliezer visited the temple construction site often—almost daily. But always, when he left the site, nagging doubts clamored in his head. Many days he would return home in a dark mood. What had he done?

The construction of the temple was the talk of the world. WNN carried on-site daily reports of the progress. In the meantime, plans were being made in anticipation of the new temple's dedication. Young rabbis went through elaborate training so that they would be qualified to minister in the temple once construction was completed. All of the necessary utensils and instruments for the offering of the daily sacrifice and oblation were now prepared.

Finally, after many months, the last stone was laid and the final touches added to the most famous building project the world had witnessed in two thousand years. Dignitaries from all over the globe were arriving almost daily to take place in the dedication festivities. Tourism was at an all-time high. Everyone who was anyone wanted to be in Jerusalem for this momentous occasion. Even the Pope had announced his intention to attend.

Chapter **12**

Things were never the same for the Freemans after they attended the teaching service conducted by Roger Cornell that night a year or so ago. Following that night, David just couldn't learn enough about the prophecies of the Bible! In his studies, he discovered that Roger had only scratched the surface in his presentation that evening.

David and Sharon began reading the books Roger had written and listened to the many tapes he had produced. They learned about the one-world government prophesied in the Bible, and they found out that the words *New World Order* were actually written in Latin on the back of the U.S. one-dollar bill. Boy, was that a wake-up call! They also learned about the World Court system that was being set up even then.

When Sharon first read the prophecy that a Jewish temple would be built during the endtimes, she was amazed. There had not been a Jewish temple since 70 A.D.; yet, she was daily witnessing the building of the prophesied temple by television! To personally experience the fulfillment of these ancient prophecies was simply astounding. It also created a level of faith in God's Word that she had previously known nothing about.

David and Sharon now discovered from the prophecies of the Bible that many of the trends of their modern society, which they had thought were good, actually would lead to horrible consequences. For example, Sharon originally had been very excited about all the religions forsaking their doctrinal differences and coming together as one. "It would be so nice for everyone to just get along," she had said. But she had no idea that the Bible prophesied that very development for the endtimes. When she realized that this global spirituality movement would be headed by the satanically inspired False Prophet, she was appalled. Because of her ignorance of God's Word, she had been duped into supporting something that was inspired by satan himself! By God's help, she decided, she would never let that happen again!

As a result of the global steps toward disarmament, the United States was rapidly downsizing its military. In due course, David received a letter from his division that made his heart leap.

"Because of recent advances toward global peace and security, the U.S. Military Forces will be reducing its size by one-half. In order to facilitate this development, we are offering early retirement to those of you who might be interested. Your pension will be less than if you served full term, but it will become effective immediately upon termination of active duty."

David couldn't place the call to Sharon fast enough. He had been praying that God would somehow make a way for him to get out of military service. Since he had come to understand what was really going on in the world, all of his priorities had changed. But he wasn't sure how Sharon would feel about this new possibility.

"Hello," Sharon answered.

"Hi, sweetheart. How are you doing?" David asked.

Sharon was surprised that he was calling during daytime hours. "What are you doing calling at this time of the day?" she inquired, hoping nothing was wrong.

"Well, something special has developed that I just couldn't wait to talk to you about. I received a letter today informing me that the military is going to be reducing its size by fifty percent due to Arachev's global disarmament program," David explained tentatively, hoping she would not be upset.

"Oh, David! That's wonderful!" Sharon exclaimed. "I've been praying that God would make a way for you to get out of the military!"

"You have?" David questioned excitedly. "I've been praying for the exact same thing! So you don't mind if I file the paperwork to leave immediately?" David asked. "I was a little concerned that you might be upset that the pension won't be as large as if I stayed in for my full term."

"David, that doesn't matter to me anymore. We are in the endtimes. We've both been praying, and now God has answered our prayer. You don't think He would lead us into His will and not provide for our needs, do you?" Sharon asked bravely.

"No, of course not," David agreed, a little ashamed that he had been so lacking in faith.

"Do you have any idea what you want to do when you get out?" Sharon inquired.

"Actually, I have been praying about something that I think God may want us to do. But you'll have to wait till I get home for me to tell you about it," David explained.

"Well, okay," Sharon agreed. "If I have to wait, I guess I won't die. When will you be home?"

"According to these forms, if my discharge is approved, I could be home in thirty days," David replied.

"Oh, David, I just know your discharge will be accepted! I know it because I believe God has a special plan for our lives. Darling, don't let me keep you on this phone. Go get those papers filed!" Sharon said excitedly. "I'll be praying."

Two weeks later, David's commander called him into his office. "Officer Freeman, I have something for you." He handed David an official-looking envelope. "Officer, it looks like you'll be leaving us. I'm sorry to lose you. You've performed notably for your country."

"Thank you, sir," David replied. "It's been an honor to serve in your unit. I appreciate everything you have done for me and for my family. It's just that my priorities have changed over the last year or so. Spiritual things have become much more important in my life."

"Yes, I've noticed that. Perhaps I, too, need to give a little more attention to that area of life," Commander Tims replied. "Good luck to you."

"And God bless you, Commander," David said sincerely.

As soon as he stepped outside Commander Tim's office, David ripped open the envelope. He already knew what it said, but he didn't know his actual release date. His eyes quickly scanned the paper. "One week from today!" David whooped. "Wow!" He walked—well, actually he ran—to the nearest telephone. He had to call Sharon! When she answered, David shouted in her ear, "One week from today, baby! One week from today!"

"You got your release?" Sharon asked.

"I got my release, and I'll be home one week from today!" David just couldn't contain his joy.

"Oh, that's wonderful. That's so wonderful!" David could hear that Sharon was weeping for joy on the other end of the line.

When Sharon and the kids picked David up at the Cincinnati Airport, the reunion was so sweet. Little Misty said, "Daddy, how long do you get to stay home this time?"

"Darling, I get to stay home from now on. I don't ever have to leave again," he replied. He could hardly believe his own words.

Misty hugged him tightly. "Yea!" she cheered. "I've been praying that I could have a full-time dad like the other kids. God answered!"

David spent the day playing with the children. That evening Sharon's mother showed up at the door. "Well hello, Mom," David greeted her. "I didn't know you were coming over."

"I'm here to take care of the children while you and Sharon go out for dinner. I understand that you have something very important to tell her," she explained.

David turned to see Sharon standing in the doorway with that mischievous grin on her face. It was very obvious that she would not be waiting till tomorrow to hear the plans that he had promised to share with her. He chuckled.

Less than a half hour later, David headed the car toward the small lakeside restaurant where he knew they could talk undisturbed. He reached over to take Sharon's hand in his own. He didn't remember ever feeling this right in his entire life. He couldn't completely explain how he knew, but he was completely certain that his life was being directed by God Himself. What a secure and exhilarating feeling!

At the restaurant, Sharon ordered grilled salmon, and David ordered steak. When the waitress left, Sharon looked at him and said, "Don't make me wait any longer. What are you thinking about for our future?"

David smiled as he began, "Sharon, I didn't mean to keep you in suspense. But this is so important, I wanted to have time to really bare my feelings to you. When I heard Roger Cornell's first sermon on prophecy, I was very deeply affected. Of course, I know that you were as well. While away from you and the kids, I've had time to go through all of Roger's material and also study a lot in the Bible. Sharon, I believe these prophecies to the very core of my being. There are just too many incredibly accurate fulfillments for them to be coincidental.

"I am totally convinced that we are in the endtimes right now. Since that it true, I can't stand the thought of giving the rest of my life to selfish pursuits. Sharon, I really want to devote the rest of my life to working for the Kingdom of God."

Sharon's eyes were brimming with tears. She was so proud to hear what David was saying. She said to him, "Darling, I feel exactly the same way. The temporary things of this world simply don't matter to me anymore. Do you have a specific area of God's work in mind?"

"Yes, actually, I do," David admitted. "You know how much understanding the prophecies has done for us. I feel like God is calling us to spend the rest of our lives helping others to understand these same things."

"Oh, David, that is wonderful! I would love for us to be able to help others in that way. But how do we go about this?" Sharon asked, puzzled.

"I've been giving that a lot of thought," David said slowly, "and I think I know what we are supposed to do. Did you notice how swamped with people Roger was the night we went to hear him? It was like there wasn't enough of him to go around. I believe God is calling us to begin working with Roger's ministry. Together we could reach twice as many people. You know, we wouldn't have to make a lot of money, since we have an income from my military pension. It's like God has arranged everything so that we can do this work."

Sharon was growing more and more excited! She could see it all in her mind. They could write letters, duplicate tapes, help set up conferences...there was just an endless number of things they could do!

The next day David placed the call to Roger Cornell in Texas and discussed with him what he felt on his heart. Roger immediately responded, "My wife and I have been so overwhelmed. We have just being praying that God would send someone to help us with this work. I'm sure your calling me is an answer to prayer."

The "For Sale" sign went up in the front yard the very next day. Sharon hated to leave family and friends, but what a thrill she felt at beginning to fulfill the very purpose for which she was born! She had never experienced such joy and peace in her entire life.

One week after the sign went up, a nice family came to look at their house. It seemed to be everything they needed. Sharon had to admit that it seemed awfully final when they said, "We'll take it." Nevertheless, her peace and joy remained at seeing God's plan for their lives coming together!

One month later, David and Sharon kissed family and friends good-bye. David drove the rented moving van, and Sharon followed behind in the family car. There was a song in David's heart as he drove toward Dallas, Texas, and his life's destiny.

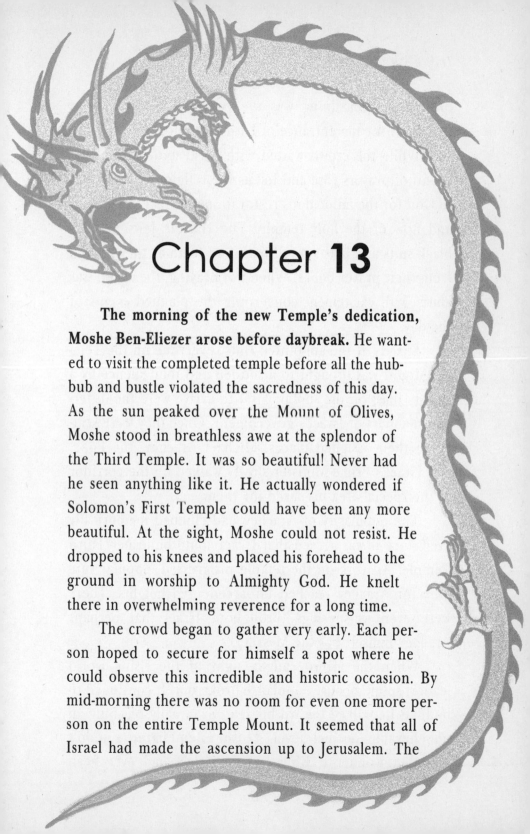

Chapter 13

The morning of the new Temple's dedication, Moshe Ben-Eliezer arose before daybreak. He wanted to visit the completed temple before all the hubbub and bustle violated the sacredness of this day. As the sun peaked over the Mount of Olives, Moshe stood in breathless awe at the splendor of the Third Temple. It was so beautiful! Never had he seen anything like it. He actually wondered if Solomon's First Temple could have been any more beautiful. At the sight, Moshe could not resist. He dropped to his knees and placed his forehead to the ground in worship to Almighty God. He knelt there in overwhelming reverence for a long time.

The crowd began to gather very early. Each person hoped to secure for himself a spot where he could observe this incredible and historic occasion. By mid-morning there was no room for even one more person on the entire Temple Mount. It seemed that all of Israel had made the ascension up to Jerusalem. The only access remaining was the corridor that had been roped off for the entrance of Israel's dignitaries.

While the crowd waited with great anticipation, the sound of prayers rose and fell as the religious gave thanks to God for the miraculous restoration of Israel to her land and now of the holy temple. The Hasidic Jews in their black suits and hats swayed back and forth as they recited from their prayer books. When not praying, the crowd was abuzz with excitement concerning the planned events of the day.

Exactly at the appointed time, everyone on the Temple Mount was brought to a sudden and total silence by a mighty blast on the shofar. First to arrive were the different members of Israel's government. Once they were seated in their assigned places, Michael Arachev, the Pope, and Israel's Prime Minister slowly walked up the corridor to the special area prepared for them.

The popularity of Arachev had climbed meteorically ever since it was agreed that Israel could build her Third Temple. As work on the temple progressed, popular support for Arachev reached unprecedented heights. There were even whisperings throughout Israel that perhaps Arachev himself was the Messiah.

When the crowd caught sight of the rising world leader, spontaneously, applause broke out. It continued to build as he walked toward his seat, eventually reaching an unbelievable decibel level. Moshe Ben-Eliezer couldn't help but wonder if King David himself had ever been greeted any more enthusiastically. Arachev finally had to stand and motion for the crowd to stop so that the ceremony could continue.

When the priests entered, much of the crowd stood with tears unashamedly coursing down their faces. Many had hoped to someday witness this occasion, but most had not dared to believe that they actually ever would. The Levites, blowing on their silver trumpets, led the way. The priests chosen to assist in the ceremony came next. They were carrying the vessels and utensils that would be dedicated to God's service, along with the temple itself. Then came the High Priest. As Israel's highest religious authority, he would preside over the temple dedication.

When the last part of the procession appeared, a murmur swept through the crowd. Many were surprised by what they saw. Several of the young priests were leading a calf along behind the High Priest. "They're actually going to offer an animal sacrifice?" someone inquired.

"Well, of course," came the reply. "That's what was done at the dedication of the First and Second Temples. Why should the dedication of the Third Temple be any different?"

Another voice was heard to say, "But this is the 21st Century! What about the animals? Animals have rights, too!"

Moshe Ben-Eliezer could not resist glancing at Michael Arachev as the calf was dragged toward the place of sacrifice. Moshe was sure he detected a shadow of disapproval crossing the world leader's face. But then it was quickly gone.

Once everyone had taken their appropriate positions, the newly formed Temple Choir began to sing. The songs of praise and worship that filled the air were absolutely beautiful. *This is what we have struggled for over the past two thousand years. This is what we were dreaming of each Passover when we would in unison say, "Next year in Jerusalem." This is the hope that kept us clinging to life during the darkest days of Hitler's horrible holocaust,* Moshe thought.

As the choir finished its last song, the priests moved into position to begin the offering of the sacrifice. Each of them had gone through the elaborate process of purification from contact with a dead body. Each priest was dressed in the linen garments that had been carefully made according to the instruction given to Moses by God on Mount Sinai. On each priestly forehead was the required frontlet inscribed with the words, HOLINESS UNTO THE LORD.

Several of the strong young priests led the calf toward the brazen altar. Together, as they had been trained, they flipped the calf to the ground, binding the front feet and the hind feet securely together. Quickly they hoisted the calf onto the brazen altar. The animal struggled momentarily, then lay still.

High Priest Cohen approached the altar brandishing the long sacrificial knife that was dedicated to the temple worship. He was very much aware that the attention of the entire world was upon him at this moment, and he fully understood the implications of what he was preparing to do. The debate over the planned sacrifice of a calf had become more heated in the last few days. The High Priest felt nothing but contempt for the hypocrisy of those animal rights activists who crusaded against the killing of animals while at the same time championing the cause of abortion. In his opinion, they were "straining at a gnat and swallowing a camel"! High Priest Cohen believed today's resumption of sacrifices, after two thousand years, marked the completion of Israel's long journey back to the holy nation God had intended her to be. This would surely serve to trigger the appearance of Messiah Himself.

As High Priest Cohen made final preparations to perform the sacrifice, his eyes swept over Arachev and Pope Peter II. Both of their faces held the perpetual inscrutable mask that politicians learn to wear. But the High Priest read their eyes, and what he saw there was strong disapproval. Although both Arachev and the Pope postured as Israel's friends, High Priest Cohen suddenly had a strong premonition that this unholy alliance between the world's foremost political leader and its most influential religious leader would someday spell disaster for the nation of Israel.

As High Priest Cohen stood beside the brazen altar in his beautiful temple garments with the fair miter upon his head, the frightened animal's eyes rolled wildly about. Another senior priest, Rabbi Akiba, stood beside the High

Priest holding the basin with which to catch the blood of the sacrifice.

When High Priest Cohen raised the long knife skyward, a holy hush swept over the entire congregation. Every photographer present trained his camera on the dramatic historic scene. The television cameras from WNN zoomed in on the calf, capturing the entire scope of the unfolding drama. All around the world, people huddled around television sets to watch this first Jewish temple sacrifice in two thousand years.

Suddenly the priest's arm swept downward, cutting cleanly through the jugular vein of the calf. It struggled and thrashed violently for a few moments, then lay still. Rabbi Akiba positioned the basin beneath the calf's throat as the blood began to gurgle from the animal. Some in the crowd chanted prayers, some averted their eyes in abhorrence, and many felt that they were going to be sick. *This*, Moshe Ben-Eliezer thought, *is going to take some getting used to*.

Moshe and many others in the crowd watched expectantly, believing that fire from God would fall out of Heaven upon the sacrifice as it had at the dedication of Solomon's First Temple. When it didn't immediately happen, the sick feeling returned to the pit of Moshe's stomach. "Perhaps God is not involved in this compromise plan after all," he muttered.

Suddenly, Pope Peter II stood up and walked forward to stand in front of the sacrifice. Raising his hand toward

Heaven, the Pope, in a dramatic gesture, swept his arm downward toward the sacrifice. To Moshe's absolute astonishment, fire came swooping from the sky and consumed the sacrifice. Every person on the Temple Mount shouted and praised God for this incredible show of His approval at the dedication of the Third Temple. Both men and women wept openly as they drank in the supernatural phenomenon that had unfolded before their eyes. Moshe stood in open amazement.

Under the incredible inspiration of the moment, even the High Priest departed from the predetermined schedule and asked the Pope to pray the prayer of dedication for the Third Temple. It just seemed like the right thing to do.

As Pope Peter stepped forward in his flowing white robes, the impressive staff in his hand, he looked every bit the part of a prophet. Then he proceeded to pray like one, too!

"O great God of the universe, thank You for bringing peace to the earth. Thank You for the great leader, which You have sent, Michael Arachev, and thank You for the building of this house of God. This is not merely a place for Jewish worship. You have shown this day that this will indeed be a house of prayer for all nations. Truly You have removed the enmity from among the nations. Even now we are in the process of beating swords into plowshares and spears into pruning hooks. We are certain that soon the lion will lie down with the lamb, and the bear and cow shall feed safely together. We thank You, O Lord, for these things that You have wrought, and we pledge to follow the direction in which Your Spirit leads. Now we dedicate this house to You. May it serve to make us all one, whether we are Jewish, Christian, Muslim, or Buddhist. Join Your children together as You intended from the beginning. We give You honor, praise, and glory, now and forever, amen."

The thousands on the Temple Mount broke into spontaneous worship. It continued to surge over the crowd in waves for quite a long time.

Finally the High Priest stepped forward to complete the prescribed ritual. The putrid smoke from the burning flesh of the sacrificial calf wafted over the Temple Mount, burning eyes and choking those who breathed in the fumes. Moshe Ben-Eliezer thought it was the most wonderful smell he had ever experienced. It was the scent of Israel returning to the offering of sacrifices as she had been instructed to perform.

The High Priest carried the basin of blood everywhere he moved. This was necessary because the basin was pointed on the bottom. It was purposely designed in this fashion so that the priest could never set it down. The motion of the priest's body ensured that the blood would be moving at all times. This, in turn, kept the blood from clotting, which would make it unfit as an offering for sin. Then the High Priest dipped the thumb of his right hand in the blood. He placed blood on his right ear and on his right big toe as instructed in the Law of Moses. After this, blood was placed on the four cornerposts of the brazen altar.

The next event in the ceremony was at the beautiful fountain called the brazen laver. It was here that the priest was required to wash himself lest he be killed by God when he entered the Holy Place. Carefully, High Priest Cohen washed, then prepared to enter the Holy Place.

Once the High Priest entered through the veil leading into the Holy Place, he was no longer visible to the people. Inside, he lit the seven candles on a beautiful candelabra. This candelabra had been captured by the Roman General Titus in 70 A.D. when he had conquered Jerusalem. The Pope had thrilled the entire nation of Israel when he announced it had been found in one of the secret chambers of the Vatican. As a gesture of goodwill, he had presented it to the nation of Israel one week before the Third Temple dedication.

The candelabra was the only source of light permitted in the Holy Place. After lighting it, the High Priest could see to eat of the shewbread from the table of shewbread and to offer the required spices on the altar of incense. This was done as praise and worship to God.

Once the service of the Holy Place was accomplished, High Priest Cohen moved toward the Holiest of Holies. With great apprehension, he pushed through the veil that separated the Holy Place from the Holiest of Holies. Some priests had been killed by God during the First and Second

Temple eras when they had entered into the Holiest of Holies in an unholy or inappropriate way. As soon as he reached the other side, the High Priest began to dip his fingers into the blood that had been taken from the altar of sacrifice.

Since the Ark of the Covenant had never been found, a beautiful cabinet had been built as a substitute. One of Israel's finest sculptors had chiseled the Ten Command-ments into two tablets of granite, and they had been placed inside. The lid for the cabinet had been built in the form of a chair, replicating the mercy seat of the Ark of the Covenant.

On the original Ark of the Covenant, the mercy seat served as its lid, covering the two stones containing the Ten Commandments, the pot of manna, and Aaron's rod that budded. In ancient times, anyone who looked upon the commandments of God would immediately die. The blood had to be sprinkled on the mercy seat in order to shield sinful man from the righteous commandments of God. Two molded cherubim joined their wings overlook-ing the mercy seat as though hovering over the very pres-ence of God.

The High Priest was careful to sprinkle the replica of the mercy seat very liberally. After all, this had not been done for 26 hundred years.

When High Priest Cohen reappeared into the outer court where the congregation was waiting, a great shout arose from the worshipers. The choir started to sing its rousing closing anthem.

Before dismissal, the presiding priest announced to the congregation that the daily sacrifice would be offered the next morning at 7 a.m. "The daily sacrifice?!" a woman near Moshe exclaimed. "Do you mean they are going to kill these animals every day?"

"Certainly," Moshe answered her. "That's the way they did in the old days, and that's the way we should do it now."

"I think this temple thing and these sacrifices are going to cause trouble," the woman said with considerable trepidation in her voice.

"It will be all right," Moshe assured her. But in his heart he wasn't at all sure himself.

On one hand, Moshe was filled with wonderment at all the things he had witnessed this day. And yet, on the other hand, something within him cried out, "It's not right! It's not right!"

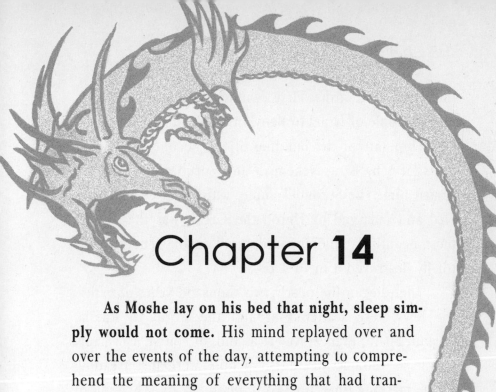

Chapter 14

As Moshe lay on his bed that night, sleep simply would not come. His mind replayed over and over the events of the day, attempting to comprehend the meaning of everything that had transpired. His clock struck 1 a.m., 2 a.m., and then 3 a.m. Still his eyes stared at the ceiling. His mind scanned the events of Israel's history as though the past could somehow illuminate the events of the present and provide clues concerning the future.

He thought about the dedication of Israel's First Temple by King Solomon. The ancient account of that grandiose event had always absolutely fascinated him. Solomon's eloquent prayer, fire falling from Heaven to consume the sacrifice, and the glory cloud that filled the temple at that first dedication enthralled him.

Then he recalled all of Israel's backsliding, which eventually resulted in God's judgment in the form of the destruction of that First Temple and the carrying away of the people of Israel to Babylon by Nebuchadnezzar.

Thoughts of the building of the Second Temple 70 years later by Ezra, Nehemiah and Zerubbabel then consumed him. The Second Temple, which had been remodeled and enlarged by Herod the Great, was the world's most beautiful building until the Roman General Titus totally destroyed it in 70 A.D.

Then began the nearly two thousand years of exile— the Jews were scattered around the world to Russia, Poland, Spain, France, America, and, of course, Germany. It was as though the Jewish people were just treading water, marking time, for two thousand years. Then, all of a sudden, the horrible holocaust. Afterwards, Jews began heading for the land of Israel from all over the globe. Against all odds and in spite of world opposition, the modern state of Israel was born in 1948. It was certainly the breathing of new life into the valley of dry bones prophesied in Ezekiel 37. Since 1948, Moshe had watched as bone came against bone and joint against joint. Then muscle and skin came upon the bones until, finally, the reformed nation began to breathe.

And now this. The long dreamed-of Third Temple was complete. Yet there were so many things Moshe couldn't understand. How could Israel leave the Dome of the Rock and the Al Aqsa mosque on God's holy mountain? To him it was idolatry and an abomination. Yet many were hailing this as the beginning of the Kingdom of God. Rumors

were rampant concerning the imminent appearance of the
Messiah. Even today many were suggesting that Michael
Arachev, the chief architect of the New World Order, was
surely the Messiah.

Then there was the Pope actually participating in the
sacrifice of an animal by pulling down fire from Heaven. It
was hard to criticize such a miracle. Yet Christians claimed
that the death of Jesus was the sacrifice that ended all sacrifices. Was Pope Peter actually willing to disregard the
New Testament for the sake of his beloved global spirituality? It was as though nothing was sacred anymore for
either Jew or Christian. Everything was being offered on
the altar of Arachev's sacred New World Order and the
new Global Interfaithism! Moshe shook his head. It was all
so confusing!

Outside, the birds began to sing. Moshe realized the
sun would soon dawn over the Mount of Olives. But still
sleep did not come. When one experiences the dream of
an entire lifetime, well, there are some things more important than sleep.

Moshe wanted to witness the first morning sacrifice
in two thousand years. He rose from bed, ate a quick bite
of breakfast, and headed for the Temple Mount.

To his consternation, several environmentalists and
animal rights activists had chosen to attend the morning
sacrificial ceremony as well. Moshe saw them discussing the
proceedings in a very angry way. He figured it wouldn't
take long for them to cause trouble. He was right.

By that evening, the media were reporting that the environmentalists and animal rights activists were actually picketing on the Temple Mount itself. They had filed suit against the Temple Institute in an attempt to stop the daily sacrifice of innocent animals. An official protest also had been filed with the United Nations.

Soon the animal sacrifice dispute developed into a full-blown world crisis. The world news agencies, with WNN leading the way, were carrying updates on the crisis every hour on the hour. Pressure was building rapidly for Israel to put a stop to the practice.

Thousands of e-mails and faxes poured into Michael Arachev's offices, demanding that he somehow resolve this absolutely unacceptable situation:

"We thought you were an environmentalist."

"We helped you to power."

"These animal sacrifices are 21st Century barbarism."

He had dealt with so many other crises. Surely he could provide a satisfactory solution to this dilemma. Arachev announced that there would be a press conference on the Temple steps at noon the next day.

The Pope had remained in Jerusalem after the Temple dedication in order to meet with Jews, Muslims, and Christians for an ecumenical celebration. After his astonishing miracle of pulling fire down from Heaven to consume the sacrifice at the Temple dedication, everyone was treating him almost as though he were a deity. Several leading papers in Israel had carried articles speculating as to whether the Pope was the promised Elijah that was to come as the forerunner of the Messiah. After all, hadn't Elijah pulled down fire from Heaven?

Thus it was no surprise that when Arachev arrived for the press conference, the Pope was at his side. These two leaders, the world's most respected political leader and the foremost religious leader, had led the way so far into what was finally looking like a genuine New World Order. Now, how would they deal with this latest impasse? The Jews had dreamed of restoring temple worship and sacrifice for two thousand years. To accept that the sacrifices could be stopped as soon as they were started would be difficult indeed. On the other hand, everyone knew how powerful the animal rights activists had become in world politics. Finding a solution wasn't going to be easy.

Michael Arachev, as his manner was, confidently strode to the microphone and immediately took control of the situation. "Many of you have been concerned about the offering of animals in the new Jewish temple. I share your concern. At the same time, we all know that, in the days of the First and Second Temples, this was an integral part of the Jewish religion. So, is there a compromise? Yes, I'm happy to announce that there is a solution to this conflict.

"Considering recent events, many have been asking if I could possibly be the promised Messiah. I'm sure each of you have read some of the articles in the press speculating about this possibility.

"Because of the present conflict, I feel the time has come to acknowledge what many of you have known instinctively for some time. I am the promised one! And I have come to lead the Jewish nation and the entire world into a new era of peace and security." Arachev smiled briefly. "As for the present issue, of course animals no longer need to be sacrificed. Your Messiah is here!"

Everyone's jaw dropped. A space of a few seconds passed as everyone attempted to absorb this announcement. Then the crowd began to applaud. Waves of clapping built like a huge tidal wave until it could be heard across the entire city of Jerusalem.

Someone in the crowd begin to chant, "Messiah, Messiah, Arachev, Messiah." Soon the entire crowd picked up the refrain: "Arachev, Messiah, Arachev, Messiah."

The cameras of WNN swept over the chanting, adoring crowd—capturing this mind-boggling development and broadcasting it to the masses around the world. When the camera returned to Michael Arachev, he stood beaming, drinking in the adulation of the people.

Then the cameras' eyes slid to Pope Peter II. How would he react to this stunning claim by Arachev to being the Messiah? Realizing that the people and the world were looking to him for guidance, the Pope swept his arm in a huge arc toward Arachev. Peter II's words carried the authority of a prophet: "The Messiah for this time—a leader sent from God—Messiah Arachev—receive him!"

The thunderous applause and shouts began all over again. "Messiah Arachev, Messiah Arachev," the crowd chanted. "Peter II is his prophet. Peter II is Elijah."

Much later, when the worship and adulation finally subsided, questions immediately started to come from the press corps as they surged forward toward the podium.

Q. "Mr. Arachev, how long have you known that you were the Messiah?"

A. "For many years now. Once I realized that I was destined to bring peace to the earth, my special calling soon became evident to me."

Q. To his holiness, Pope Peter II: "What do you make of this claim by Arachev to being the Messiah?"

A. "I've known for a long time that God had a special mission for Michael Arachev. You may recall that my predecessor, back in 1992, suggested that Mr. Arachev would make the ideal leader for a united Europe. The world must now follow his leadership. The promised time for which all of us have waited has now arrived."

Q. "Michael Arachev, what will happen to those who refuse to acknowledge your role as the ordained leader of the world?"

A. "They will eventually follow. We have a plan to reeducate any who do not yet understand the absolute necessity of the unity of mankind. I'm sure they will soon realize that our plan is for their good and that of the entire world."

Many questions later, Arachev made his final statement. "Ladies and gentleman of the press corps, this has been a very eventful day for all of us. You probably have many other questions. However, from now on, I will address the World Community on a regular basis. Those things you need to know will be revealed when the time is right. I'm counting on your help as we lead our world into one thousand years of peace and security. God bless you, and good evening."

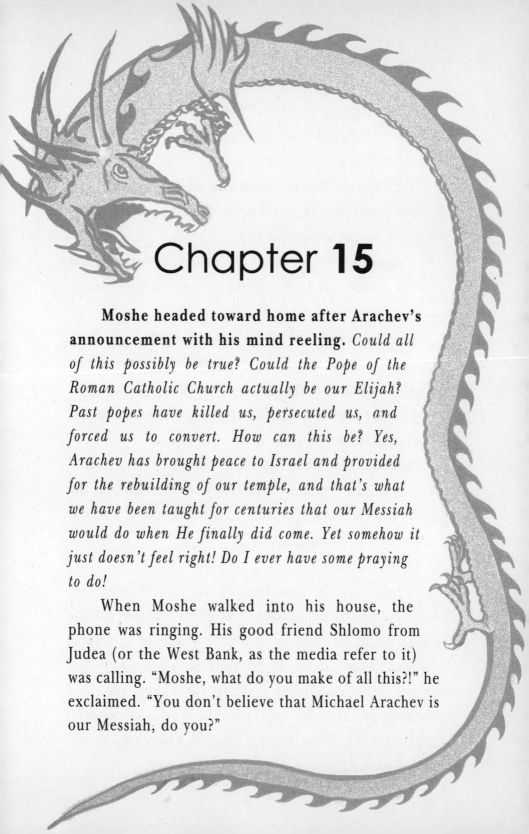

Chapter 15

Moshe headed toward home after Arachev's announcement with his mind reeling. *Could all of this possibly be true? Could the Pope of the Roman Catholic Church actually be our Elijah? Past popes have killed us, persecuted us, and forced us to convert. How can this be? Yes, Arachev has brought peace to Israel and provided for the rebuilding of our temple, and that's what we have been taught for centuries that our Messiah would do when He finally did come. Yet somehow it just doesn't feel right! Do I ever have some praying to do!*

When Moshe walked into his house, the phone was ringing. His good friend Shlomo from Judea (or the West Bank, as the media refer to it) was calling. "Moshe, what do you make of all this?!" he exclaimed. "You don't believe that Michael Arachev is our Messiah, do you?"

"Well, I just don't know," Moshe said pensively. "He has helped bring peace to Israel, and he did clear the way for the building of our temple."

"But, Moshe, they're saying that Buddhists, Muslims, Christians, and Jews all worship the same God! You surely don't believe that either, do you?"

"Shlomo, we've had three thousand years of wars and religious conflict. It really would be nice to have peace. Maybe we need to be more broad-minded."

"Wait a minute, Moshe." Shlomo couldn't believe his ears. "You know the Scriptures say that when the true Messiah comes there will be one Lord and His name one. He will bring us the truth, not some kind of global hodgepodge!"

"Shlomo, you may well be right. By the way, I'm glad you called. There's one thing that's been bothering me quite a bit ever since the press conference. I feel I owe it to you to say something about it."

"What's that?"

"I have this Christian friend who, several years ago, told me all of this would happen someday. He told me the Temple would be built north of the Dome of the Rock, leaving the Dome in the Outer Court. He also told me that animal sacrifices would be resumed for a short time and then stopped. He also said that the world leader who stopped the sacrifices would stand in the Temple and claim to be the Messiah."

"He told you several years ago that all of this was going to happen? Well, then, maybe Arachev is the Messiah!"

"No, no, no. He didn't say the one who did these things would be the Messiah. He said he would be a false messiah—the antichrist."

"That's incredible, but you know, I think I could believe it! I mean, especially since your friend told you so far in advance in such intricate detail."

"There's one more thing, which is the most important one of all. He told me that, when the antichrist stood in the Temple claiming to be the Messiah, horrible persecution would then break out against all the Jews living in Judea. Since that's where you live, I felt like I should definitely tell you about it in case it proved to be right."

"Well, everything else has proven to be right. Did your friend tell you what we who live in Judea should do?"

"Yes, actually, he did. He said that you must immediately flee into the mountains or wherever you can find a safe place. He claimed that the outbreak of violence would come so fast that if you are in your field, you should not even return to your house to get anything. He said that you must run for your life without delay!"

"Wow! I'm out in my field right now. I just used my cell phone to call you. Are you saying that I should flee from here right now?"

"That's what he said. Listen, just to be safe, why don't you take off this very moment? See if you can make it to my house, until we see whether this comes to pass. If something happens that you can't make it here, remember to just flee into the countryside and hide until you can get to safety. Shlomo, I really think you should do this right now! Keep your phone with you in case you need to call me. I'll be praying for you."

"Thanks, Moshe. I may need it. Shalom."

Shlomo nosed his Volvo onto the main road leading into Jerusalem. The checkpoint lay only ten kilometers ahead. His mind raced, planning what to do if he encountered trouble. His eyes scanned the horizon, looking for anything unusual. About three kilometers from the safety of Israeli-held territory, he saw traffic backing up in front of him. Instantly, he knew what he had to do.

He swerved onto a little-used back road that he knew would take him within about a kilometer and a half of Israel proper. The road was full of huge chuckholes. It had ceased to be used several years back. After one kilometer, two Palestinian soldiers stepped into the middle of the road, signaling him to stop. Shlomo slowed as if to stop, but at the last moment shoved the accelerator to the floor, aiming the car at first one soldier and then the other. As they dove for safety, the Volvo went careening by.

Shlomo knew that he couldn't stay with the vehicle long. Soon the hillside would be teeming with Palestinians searching for him. About half a kilometer further, he slowed the vehicle near the edge of a steep ravine. Taking only a bottle of water and his cell phone, he stuffed an old pillow between the brake and the accelerator, then jumped clear. The Volvo lunged forward, catapulting over the ravine onto the rocks 120 feet below. The Palestinian vehicles in pursuit of him were only a few hundred feet away. They were coming from the passenger side, though, so he was sure they wouldn't have seen him tumble out. He quickly hid himself where he could watch without being seen.

The tire marks on the pavement and the ridges where the Volvo had plunged off the road and over the edge were clearly visible. One of the Palestinians noticed and ordered their vehicle to stop. Gazing down to the rocks below, it was obvious to them that no one could have survived that wreck. Shlomo heard one of them say, "Dirty kike. Just what he deserved."

Shlomo waited quietly in his hiding place. It didn't take long for the Palestinians to return to their checkpoint. He lay quiet and thought. According to his calculations, he was approximately one and a half kilometers from Har Homa. Could he get there? He knew that he was facing the greatest level of danger that he had ever experienced in his life. "Dear God, be with me," he prayed quietly under his breath.

Shlomo headed cross-country in the direction of Har Homa. He decided to risk one phone call. "Moshe, this is Shlomo. What you told me turned out to be right on the money. I need help. Meet me right at the edge of Har Homa at 9 o'clock."

Moshe's voice never hesitated. "You got it. I'll be there. Look for my work vehicle." Shlomo knew that was Moshe's way of letting him know that he would be in the red panel van.

Shlomo traveled swiftly, but carefully. One careless move could mean his end. At 8:45 p.m., he approached the rendezvous point. He quickly hid himself about a hundred meters from the road. The border separating Palestinian territory from Israel proper was the only thing that stood between him and safety. He observed that the patrols monitoring the border were very frequent. Apparently they were looking for escaping settlers just like him.

Shlomo didn't have much time to plan his dash to freedom. Each time the border sentry passed, Shlomo checked his watch. They were running at two-minute intervals. This was not going to be easy. His eyes scanned Israeli territory just ahead of him. He saw no sign of Moshe, but he was absolutely sure that he was there. If he knew his friend at all, Moshe was sitting in the darkness in his van, timing the intervals of the border patrols just like he was. Five minutes till nine. Another Palestinian soldier walked by, looking around carefully as he went. At three minutes till the hour, another guard went by. Still no sign of Moshe.

Shlomo's senses were heightened by the danger that loomed just ahead. His eyes scanned the hills on the other side of the road carefully and systematically. Would Moshe make his move after the sentry passed at one minute before the hour, or would he wait until one minute after? As the next guard passed, the soldier looked right over in Shlomo's direction. Shlomo hugged the ground. *There's no way he could have seen me*, he thought. After a long hesitation, the Palestinian continued on. Every muscle in Shlomo's body now tensed for the dash through mortal danger to safety. A full minute passed. No sign of Moshe. Every second was vital! Shlomo was like a coiled spring ready to release. Still there was nothing.

What if something had happened? What if Moshe had been stopped from coming by the Israeli police because of the volatility of the area? Shlomo shoved those tormenting thoughts to the back of his mind. *No. I know Moshe. He will be here. I would trust him with my life.* For a moment, Shlomo allowed himself a wry grin. *I guess that's what I'm doing right now, isn't it?*

It was at that instant that Shlomo saw the beam of the headlights coming around the corner. *This is it!* he thought. Now everything was instinct. His legs pumped like two powerful cylinders. "Faster," he said to himself. He was weaving as he ran. It sounded like a firecracker, but Shlomo knew exactly what it was. He had heard the

123

crack of an AK-47 too many times. "Move it, move it," he screamed to himself. Out of the corner of his eye, he saw the next sentry running in his direction. Shlomo felt like he was in slow motion. He could tell that Moshe was moving along slowly, as though nothing was afoot. Yet, apparently, he had spotted Shlomo weaving through the trees and the rocks. Shlomo was about fifty feet from Moshe's red van and safety, but bullets were now whizzing all about him.

The van was now only twenty feet ahead, but it was still moving at close to twenty kilometers per hour. Maybe Moshe hadn't seen him after all. "O God, help us right now!" When Shlomo was ten feet away from the moving van, he heard the click of the latch on the side door, and then he understood. He timed his leap right for the side door. Miraculously, the door flew open, and he found himself lying gasping and exhausted on the carpeted floor. Instantly, as though it had never been opened, the door slammed shut behind him. Shlomo heard the roar of the 352 engine as Moshe buried the accelerator in the floorboard.

"All you all right?" he heard Moshe scream.

"I'm just fine," Shlomo gasped. "Thanks."

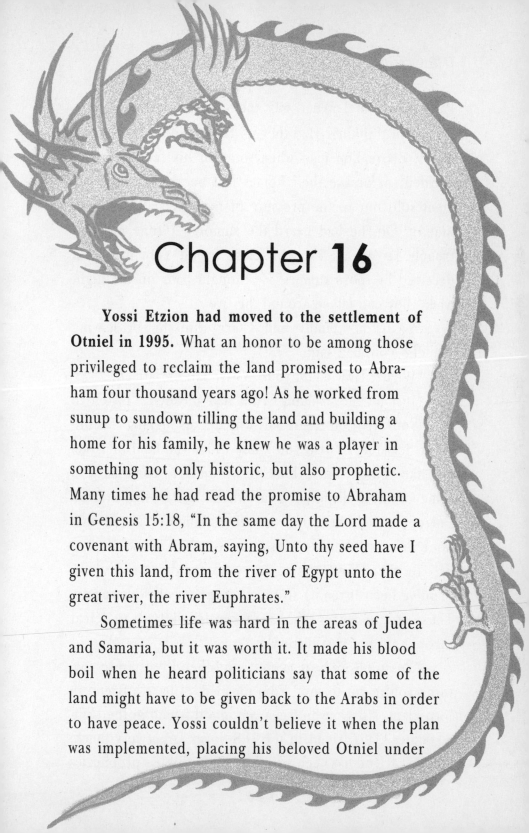

Chapter **16**

Yossi Etzion had moved to the settlement of Otniel in 1995. What an honor to be among those privileged to reclaim the land promised to Abraham four thousand years ago! As he worked from sunup to sundown tilling the land and building a home for his family, he knew he was a player in something not only historic, but also prophetic. Many times he had read the promise to Abraham in Genesis 15:18, "In the same day the Lord made a covenant with Abram, saying, Unto thy seed have I given this land, from the river of Egypt unto the great river, the river Euphrates."

Sometimes life was hard in the areas of Judea and Samaria, but it was worth it. It made his blood boil when he heard politicians say that some of the land might have to be given back to the Arabs in order to have peace. Yossi couldn't believe it when the plan was implemented, placing his beloved Otniel under

Palestinian rule! What was the godless government in Jerusalem thinking? Had they no faith at all?

It drove him mad when some of his fellow settlers decided to forsake their homes just because the government sold out to the pressure of the international community. Oh, he had heard the rumors! A time of great trouble lay ahead. Even his close friend Yoni had been deceived by those rumors. He thought back on the night when they had talked around the fire.

"Yossi, my family and I are thinking of leaving Otniel," Yoni had said.

"What?! How could you?" Yossi had exclaimed.

"Just let me explain," Yoni had pleaded. "Listen to me." Yoni went on to present why he was making this difficult decision. "Yossi, you know I love the land of Israel just like you do. But I think we will have to come back to some of these disputed areas when the Messiah arrives. I'm convinced there is a horrible slaughter ahead that none of us will be able to stop, no matter what we do."

By then, Yossi was so angry he couldn't keep silent. "You've been listening to those prophets of doom again. Those are the voices that have taken Israel down to defeat throughout her past history!"

"Yossi, please hear me out, and then I'll listen to anything you've got to say," Yoni pleaded. "I have a friend in Jerusalem, Moshe, who has a very good friend in the United States. This friend in the U.S. loves Israel very much. Moshe's friend has been a student of the Bible's prophecies for many, many years. He told Moshe several years ago what the Bible says is coming. And, Yossi, so far everything has come to pass!"

"Like what?" Yossi challenged.

"He told Moshe that Israel would trade land for peace. And it happened. Then he told him our temple would be rebuilt on the Temple Mount. That is happening now."

Yossi interrupted, "So what? We have all believed that the temple would be rebuilt."

"I know. But that's not all," Yoni continued. "He told him several years in advance that the temple would be built north of the Dome of the Rock, leaving the Dome of the Rock in the temple's outer court. Yossi, you know that none of us believed that would ever happen, but that's where they're building right now! He also said that animal sacrifices would be resumed, causing worldwide opposition by the animal rights activists. You know the debate that's raging right now over the plan to reinstitute the daily sacrifices when the temple is completed."

"But what does this have to do with your leaving our settlement?" Yossi demanded.

"That's the point," Yoni explained. "It has everything to do with it. This man also told Moshe that the Bible predicts in great detail a horrible slaughter in the area of Judea for the times immediately ahead of us now."

Yossi exploded. "All of these so-called prophecies are nothing but a plot to weaken the hands of God's people!

You know yourself how many have deserted us because of these prophecies. And besides, aren't some of these supposed prophecies from the New Testament? Why should we give those any consideration at all?!"

"But they have all come to pass!" Yoni argued. "How can we ignore them? And it looks like the ones that haven't happened yet are right on target."

"So what do the prophecies say we should do about the coming trouble?" Yossi asked.

"They say we must flee Judea. They say a horrible slaughter is coming that will sweep away all who remain," Yoni explained.

Yossi's reaction was violent. "You're just like all the rest—cowards! I thought you were the one person in the world I could count on. But no! You're just a yellow coward like the rest of the deserters!" Yossi almost spit out the bitter words, as if they were so vile he had to get them out of his mouth. "I don't care what your stupid prophecies say. My family and I will defend the holy land of Israel, and we will gladly die for this soil, if necessary. Run like a coward, if that's what you want to do. We're staying!"

Yossi's words cut like a dagger into his friend's heart. Yet Yoni knew that Yossi really believed them. "Yossi, one more thing before I go. There is a very specific event that is supposed to happen that will trigger the coming holocaust prophesied for Judea. The prophecy states that a great global leader will ascend to power. When the furor develops over the animal sacrifices, this global leader will stand in the temple, stop the sacrifices, and claim to be the Messiah. At least keep your eyes on the news, and if those things happen, get out of here!"

Yossi remembered the conversation as if it were yesterday, though it had occurred many months ago now. He had tried to put all of those superstitions out of his mind. But try as he would, sometimes he would think about them—especially when he heard the news. And especially since the Temple dedication two days ago.

Just this morning on the radio they had been discussing world reaction to the animal sacrifices. Yossi had thought to himself, *They can kill Jews. Just don't kill their beloved animals!* He understood that Michael Arachev was scheduled to hold a news conference on the Temple steps at noon today concerning the subject. Yossi decided to come back to the house at noon so he could see for himself what it was all about.

Before he headed to the field, Yossi checked his guns, his ammunition store, and the hand grenades he had purchased just in case things got really rough. He wouldn't admit to himself that the possibility of the fulfillment of the prophecies was making him nervous. But it never hurt to be sure.

At noon, when he arrived back at the house, his wife Sarah had lunch already on the table. Yossi quickly flipped on the television. The news conference was only beginning. Michael Arachev, smooth as always, began:

"Many of you have been concerned about the offering of animals in the new Jewish temple. I share your concern. At the same time, we all know that, in the days of the First and Second Temples, this was an integral part of the Jewish religion. So, is there a compromise? Yes, I'm happy to announce that there is a solution to this conflict.

"Considering recent events, many have been asking if I could possibly be the promised Messiah. I'm sure each of you have read some of the articles in the press speculating about this possibility.

"Because of the present conflict, I feel the time has come to acknowledge what many of you have known instinctively for some time. I am the promised one! And I have come to lead the Jewish nation and the entire world into a new era of peace and security. As for the present issue, of course animals no longer need to be sacrificed. Your Messiah is here!"

Thunderous applause swelled from the crowd that had gathered for the press conference. But Yossi had a horrible sickened feeling deep in the pit of his stomach. "Yossi, you're not eating your lunch," Sarah noted, concerned. "Are you all right? You look like you're becoming ill."

"No, I'm all right. But, Sarah, we could be headed for some trouble. Take the kids down to the settlement bunker, and then meet me at our assigned defense position as quickly as possible."

"Yossi, what's wrong?" Sarah cried.

"Don't ask any questions. Just do as I say!" Yossi was already running out the door.

As the afternoon wore on, unusual activity was noticed among the Palestinians—and among their military personnel, in particular. Along about evening, Yossi heard the cry from the Palestinian command post nearby. "Allahu Akbar! God is Great! God is Great! There is no other god but Allah! Death to the infidels! Death to the Jews!"

He heard the low whine of the first incoming missile. It slammed directly into the town hall where the settlement's men held their town meetings. The town hall exploded into flames. This was not merely an isolated harassment to which the settlers had become accustomed. This was all-out war!

As if out of nowhere on a given secret signal, Palestinians began to converge on Otniel. "God is great! God is great!" they screamed as they surged forward. From his defensive position above, Yossi began to pick them off one by one. When the magazine clip in one rifle was emptied, Sarah handed him a loaded one. Yossi and his fellow defenders exacted a terrible price from the attackers. But still they came. The sheer numbers were absolutely staggering! It was bone-chilling to see the fanaticism in their faces as they ran blindly forward, screaming, "God is great!"

The defenders fought valiantly, but they were severely outnumbered. The position of the advancing attackers inched slowly forward. The settlers knew that they were standing alone. There would be no Israeli army to rescue them this time. When the separation plan was implemented, they had been told in no uncertain terms that, if they chose to remain under Palestinian authority, they could not expect to be rescued in case of hostilities.

The first break in the defense line came to Yossi's left. He saw his close friend Baruch go down. They had worked in the fields together. They had helped each other build their houses. Many sabbaths were spent together dreaming of the time when Eretz Yisrael would be under total Israeli control and at peace. Yossi looked away. The whole right side of Baruch's face had been blown off.

The Arab attack was savage! The incoming fire was unrelenting. The Israeli settlers had no choice. They had to pull back their line of defense. The bloody house-to-house fighting for their settlement had begun. For every Israeli that went down, he took five Arabs with him. But they were outnumbered twenty to one!

The perimeter of their defense slowly but surely shrank, moving ever closer to that precious bunker holding their children. There they would make their last stand.

As the Palestinians reorganized themselves for their final assault, Yossi and Sarah found themselves alone for a moment. Both knew that hope was quickly vanishing. Sarah had, during many evenings, encouraged Yossi to follow Yoni out of the settlement and into safety. She had watched the fulfillment of one prophecy after another until she had no doubt that they were true. However, in the face of every argument, Yossi would always square his jaw and say, "This is our Promised Land. I will never leave it! I will die here, if necessary."

Yossi looked at the fear in Sarah's eyes. "I should have listened," he said. "I'm sorry."

Sarah smiled sweetly into his eyes, "I love you. I always have, and I always will—whatever happens. Just don't let them take me alive. I couldn't stand the horrible things they might do."

"That won't happen," Yossi promised. He paused. "But we must see about the children."

The massacre was now in full swing. Three Arabs had slipped through the back way and had reached the safehouse where the children were. A mother was pleading with one of the attackers, "Kill me, but don't kill my baby." The Arab yanked the little boy from her arms. "The only good Jew is a dead Jew," he screamed. With that, he flung the little boy into the air, catching him on the end of his bayonet. As the boy screamed in the agonies of death, the mother fell on top of him with an unearthly wail of agony. "My baby, my baby," she cried, oblivious to her own mortal danger. Then her body convulsed as the Arab's bullets brought an end to her tortured screams.

It was obvious that all was lost. Only Yossi, Sarah, their two children, and eleven other settlers huddled in the innermost bunker. The incoming fire was withering, and they were almost out of ammunition. Twenty minutes later, Yossi put the rifle to his shoulder once again. Click. It was empty.

Apparently the Arab just around the corner from the opening of the bunker heard it as well. He slowly stuck his head into the door with a look of triumph on his face. All the settlers could do was huddle helplessly in the corner of the bunker. The Palestinian pulled the pin on the grenade and slowly lobbed it into the bunker. Just before the death-dealing explosion, the cry of the fleeing Arab was heard, "God is great!"

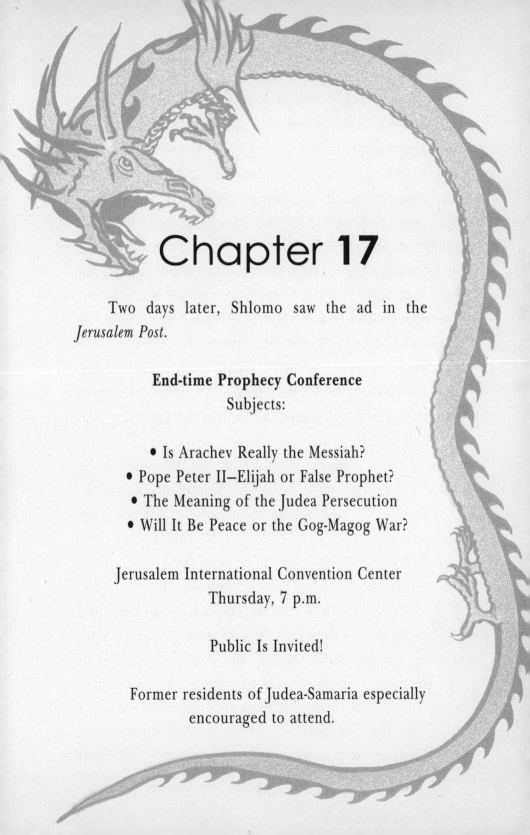

Chapter **17**

Two days later, Shlomo saw the ad in the *Jerusalem Post*.

End-time Prophecy Conference
Subjects:

* Is Arachev Really the Messiah?
* Pope Peter II—Elijah or False Prophet?
* The Meaning of the Judea Persecution
* Will It Be Peace or the Gog-Magog War?

Jerusalem International Convention Center
Thursday, 7 p.m.

Public Is Invited!

Former residents of Judea-Samaria especially
encouraged to attend.

"Moshe, look at this!" Shlomo exclaimed, showing the ad to Moshe. "Let's go see what this is all about!"

The conference was to start the next evening. Shlomo and Moshe made sure they arrived early. Even so, the Jerusalem International Convention Center was packed. They were surprised to see how many former residents of Judea and Samaria were there.

The featured speakers were two quite ordinary-looking men, but what they had to say was anything but ordinary. The power with which they spoke exceeded anything either Shlomo or Moshe had ever experienced.

The first speaker, Roger Cornell, opened with the session, "Is Arachev Really the Messiah?" Cornell took them step by step through the prophecies in the Bible concerning the Messiah.

"Micah 5:2 explicitly says that the Messiah will be born in Bethlehem—'But thou, Bethlehem Ephratah, though thou be little among the thousands of Judah, yet out of thee shall he come forth unto Me that is to be ruler in Israel; whose goings forth have been from of old, from everlasting.' Was Arachev born in Bethlehem?

"Isaiah 7:14 tells us that the Messiah will be born of a virgin—'Therefore the Lord Himself shall give you a sign; Behold, a virgin shall conceive, and bear a son, and shall call His name Immanuel.' Was Arachev born of a virgin?

"Genesis 49:10 says that the true Messiah will come from the tribe of Judah—'The sceptre shall not depart from Judah, nor a lawgiver from between his feet, until

Shiloh come; and unto Him shall the gathering of the people be.' Does Arachev come from the tribe of Judah?

"Ladies and gentlemen, the answer to every one of these questions is, absolutely not. The plain truth is that Arachev is simply not your Messiah, or mine! And if he is not the Messiah, as he claims, then what is he? He is an imposter! He is not the Messiah. He is the anti-messiah. He is not the Christ; he is the antichrist!"

Shlomo and Moshe looked nervously around the room. These were dangerous words to be speaking. Since the New World Order had gained control, such open speech was no longer tolerated. Moshe had to admit, however, that it was quite refreshing to hear someone speak plainly and with courage. It had been quite a long time since anyone had dared.

Speaker Cornell continued, "How do I know that arachev is the antichrist? Because he fulfills all the biblical prophecies concerning what the antichrist will do. Allow me to list a few.

"First, he confirmed a covenant concerning the future of Jerusalem and the Temple. You'll find that in (Daniel 9:27). Second, he came to power in the midst of a ten-nation union. Look at Daniel 7:24. Third, he caused the sacrifice and the oblation to cease, as in Daniel 9:27. And fourth, he sat in the Temple and claimed to be Messiah and God. Refer to the New Testatment Book of Second Thessalonians 2:3-4.

137

"These are just a few of the fifty prophecies concerning the antichrist and what is prophesied he will do."

By this time Shlomo's mind was racing. *It all makes sense! For one man to fulfill all of these prophecies just cannot be a coincidence.*

The second speaker, David Freeman, stepped to the podium. "I want to speak on the following subject: 'Pope Peter II—Elijah or False Prophet?'"

Both Shlomo and Moshe sat spellbound as Freeman went through the Bible's prophecies about the Holy Roman Empire. "The Holy Roman Empire was born in 800 A.D. when Pope Leo III placed the crown on the head of Charlemagne. At that time, Pope Leo III made the pronouncement, 'I now crown you emperor of the Holy Roman Empire.' You see, there were always two leaders in the Holy Roman Empire—a political leader and a spiritual leader.

"The Bible prophesies that the one-world government of the endtimes will be the final revival of the Holy Roman Empire. That's why the Book of Revelation clearly states there will be two leaders in the last-day world government—the antichrist and the false prophet.

"In the Book of Revelation chapter 13, we are told that the false prophet will pull down fire from Heaven in the sight of men and will deceive the world by means of the miracles that he will have power to do!"

Moshe looked at Shlomo and whispered, "That's exactly what happened! This is astounding!"

Freeman continued, "Revelation tells us that the false prophet will use his global influence to cause the world to give allegiance to the antichrist and his world government. If you want to know who Pope Peter II is, ladies and gentlemen, he is not Elijah. He is the false prophet!

"And now for a final word specifically for those of you who recently had to escape from Judea." Shlomo felt like Freeman was speaking directly to him.

"You were warned to flee from Judea when the antichrist stood in the temple claiming to be the Messiah. But you owe it to yourself to know the source of the prophecy that saved your life. That prophecy was recorded in Matthew 24:15-16 and was spoken by a famous man by the name of Jesus. Yes, if it were not for the prophecy of Jesus, you would have perished just like all of your friends did who refused to believe His words. Jesus actually became your Savior a few days ago. He saved your physical life. However, Jesus did not merely come to this earth to save you physically. He came so that you might have eternal life.

"My dear friends, Jesus is not only your Savior; He is also your Messiah. It was Jesus of whom the prophet Isaiah spoke in Isaiah 53:5-6: 'But He was wounded for our transgressions, He was bruised for our iniquities: the chastisement of our peace was upon Him; and with His stripes we are healed. All we like sheep have gone astray; we have turned every one to his own way; and the Lord hath laid on Him the iniquity of us all.'

"The wonderful Jewish people have ignored this messianic prophecy for too long. When Jesus was crucified almost two thousand years ago, He became the fulfillment of Isaiah 53. He became the Passover lamb that was wounded for our sins and who paid the penalty of death for each of us so that we could have eternal life.

"I know that this is a huge step for some of you, but if you would like to express your belief in Jesus Christ as your Lord and Savior, please walk to the front right now."

Moshe was stunned when he saw several hundred Israelis going forward to express their faith in Jesus as Messiah. Then he remembered Shlomo. *I wonder what he's thinking of all this?* But Moshe couldn't see him anywhere. Where had Shlomo gone? Then down near the front Moshe spotted the blue kippa his friend always wore. His hands were high in the air as he gave praise to Jesus as his Lord and his Messiah.

Oh my! Life won't be the same after this night, Moshe thought. He had to wonder where all this would ultimately lead.

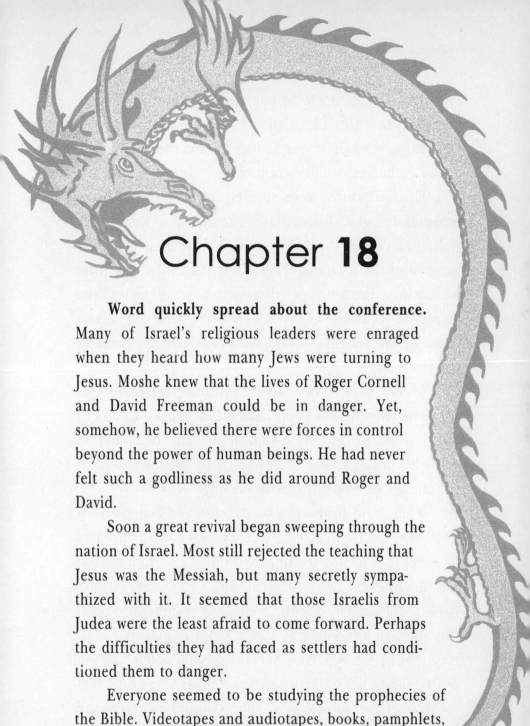

Chapter **18**

Word quickly spread about the conference.
Many of Israel's religious leaders were enraged
when they heard how many Jews were turning to
Jesus. Moshe knew that the lives of Roger Cornell
and David Freeman could be in danger. Yet,
somehow, he believed there were forces in control
beyond the power of human beings. He had never
felt such a godliness as he did around Roger and
David.

Soon a great revival began sweeping through the
nation of Israel. Most still rejected the teaching that
Jesus was the Messiah, but many secretly sympa-
thized with it. It seemed that those Israelis from
Judea were the least afraid to come forward. Perhaps
the difficulties they had faced as settlers had condi-
tioned them to danger.

Everyone seemed to be studying the prophecies of
the Bible. Videotapes and audiotapes, books, pamphlets,
and magazines were passed from person to person.

No one was supposed to be talking about these issues, but everyone was. This Christian fire was getting out of control! Roger and David seemed to be everywhere—on talk shows, in homes, at hotel conference rooms—everywhere.

The authorities were so busy with their grandiose schemes for global government that, for a while, they didn't recognize the force of the movement that had been born. As a consequence, they paid relatively little attention to these two prophets who now frequented the streets of Jerusalem. They were merely regarded as two more of the religious kooks who regularly appeared in the Holy City.

At the same time, reports of this revival and its prophetic significance swept around the world. Lovers of Israel began to contribute significant sums of money to Cornell's ministry, who then used it to fan the flames of the already blazing spiritual awakening.

When it finally dawned on Arachev and Pope Peter II how powerful the return to true biblical Christianity had become, they turned the full forces of their wrath against the movement. Laws against prophecy conferences were passed. The influence of the media was mobilized to paint this spiritual awakening as a cult and a right-wing fundamentalist hate group. However, the general public had witnessed the tactics of the mainstream press for so long that many saw right through it. Besides that, the believers had become very skilled at using the Internet to spread the good news. New websites were springing up faster than the web police were able to shut them down. A world that had been fed controlled news for so long, now hungrily devoured the unvarnished reports that were produced by the Bible Christian movement.

Arachev and Pope Peter II tried every device possible to stamp out this surging threat to their beloved New World Order, forcing the Church to go underground. It was so ironic. They had thought the Internet was the key to finally realizing their dream of one-world government. Now that same technology threatened to be the very tool used for its unraveling.

Assassination attempts were made on the lives of David, Roger, and other leaders of the revival. A few of the leaders were killed, but for the most part God granted divine protection beyond anything believers had ever experienced before. It was remarkable!

It was during this time that God began to use Roger Cornell and David Freeman to perform some incredible miracles. The modern underground Christian Church had returned to the power of 1st Century Christianity.

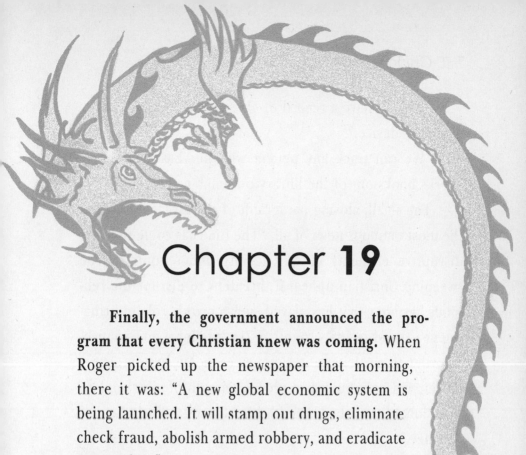

Chapter 19

Finally, the government announced the program that every Christian knew was coming. When Roger picked up the newspaper that morning, there it was: "A new global economic system is being launched. It will stamp out drugs, eliminate check fraud, abolish armed robbery, and eradicate tax evasion."

In actuality, this system was not totally new. Most people in the world had been operating practically cashless for a number of years. The big difference was that this system finally called for the elimination of cash altogether. With this new development, participation in the cashless society became mandatory.

As usual, a vast majority of human beings repeated the thinking they were being spoon-fed by the establishment media.

"The drug problem just has to be solved."

"This will stop the terrorists cold in their tracks."

"We will have a record of every person who buys any explosive device."

"We can track any person who purchases books or checks books out of the library on bomb-making."

The small, closing paragraph of the article contained the most ominous news of all. "The time has come to bring disruptive elements of our society under control. The sweeping Christian upheaval threatens to disrupt the religious harmony that has played such a pivotal role in bringing peace and security to our system of global governance. In order to participate in the new economic system, every citizen will be required to pledge an oath of allegiance to the Global Ethic, the United Nations, and to World Leader Arachev."

The enactment of this new legislation had the opposite effect from what Arachev and Pope Peter II intended. Instead of driving people away from the Bible-believing Christians, it attracted more people to them. The believers had been warning everyone for a long time that this development was coming. Consequently, when it actually happened, it merely added fuel to the fire of the Christians' faith. The stronger the opposition rose against them, the closer they drew together; the more they were persecuted, the faster they grew.

The implementation of the new system was fairly simple. In truth, the technology to run such a program had been available for a long time. Public resistance had been the only thing that stood in its way.

Arachev and Pope Peter II agreed that the threat to the New World Order was serious enough to mandate coercive force. They could sense the tide of society shifting from allegiance to their system of global government and global spirituality to the Christian groundswell. They agreed that it was now or never for their New World Order. If they didn't stamp out the movement headed by Roger Cornell and David Freeman now, everything the globalists had worked so hard to achieve for the past one hundred years would go down the drain. The time for strong, resolute action had come.

The first step was to issue a Personal Identification Number to every person on earth. For Americans, for instance, this would be their Social Security number. While this was being accomplished, the global computer system that had been under development for several years would have to be prepared for number validating. This would not be difficult since the necessary software already existed. They would employ the same method that was used to check the validity of a credit card. If a card was overcharged, the message merely came back: Transaction declined.

That's the way this new system would work. If a person had not cleared the validation process, any attempt to conduct financial transactions would trigger the "transaction declined" message. Arachev and Peter II were sure that every person would soon bow to the will of the World Community. After all, money was the bottom line. When people couldn't eat or feed their families, they would submit.

It was January 1 when the letters arrived at the mailboxes of every citizen under the New World Order's control. "Our new system of safety and security has now been tested and is ready for implementation. This system will provide you and your family with absolute security against terrorism, theft, drugs, and religious proselytizing. Won't it be wonderful to live in a society where the drug trade is eradicated, bank robberies are impossible, personal muggings are a thing of the past, and you never have to worry about having forgotten your wallet?"

The letter continued, "All that each citizen will need for the implementation of this global security system will be his own validated Personal Identification Number. The time of the appointment for you and your family to receive your number validation will be sent to you within the next three days. You should be at your local courthouse by 9 a.m. on your assigned date. This new cashless system of safety and security will take effect on March 1st. Make sure all money is deposited in your bank account before that date. Any money not transferred into electronic funds will be worthless after that time. You should take special care to assist the elderly and the young in making this transition, as it would be tragic if people lost their life savings because of negligence." The letter was signed, "Global President, Michael Arachev."

When people around the world received this seemingly innocent letter, reactions were mixed. Some hailed this as a long overdue development. "The only people against a system like this are the criminals. If you don't have anything to hide, what's the problem?"

Of course, the privacy advocates opposed it. But there are always those who are paranoid—those who see a bear behind every bush. Heated arguments about "Big Brother" and the encroachment of big government were heard on all the talk shows. But the media "spin doctors" did their job..."What privacy? Since the Internet, everything is known about everybody anyway. Get used to it!"

In the meantime, the Bible-believing Christians were experiencing unprecedented mobilization. "The Letter," as it came to be called, became the Christian's foremost witnessing tool. Bible studies were in progress around the world all through the day—morning, noon, and night. The subject was the same at every study. "The Letter" would be laid on the table and the Bible opened to Revelation 13:16-17: "And he causeth all, both small and great, rich and poor, free and bond, to receive a mark in their right hand, or in their foreheads: and that no man might buy or sell, save he that had the mark, or the name of the beast, or the number of his name."

It was shown in the Bible that anyone who took this number, called the "mark of the beast," would be forever lost. People were persuaded by the thousands to refuse the mark of the antichrist and, instead, to receive the name of the real Christ through baptism. During this month of "The Letter," more new Christians were baptized than in any other month in the entire history of the world. The advance of biblical Christianity was nothing short of remarkable!

When John and Melinda Snyder arrived at the county courthouse, the line was quite long. Melinda had not been at all excited about having a computer chip implanted under her skin. She could see the advantages of it when it came to her children. If they were ever kidnapped or lost, they could be immediately located by global positioning satellites. She did like that feature of this new system. The thing that bothered her most was memories of sermons she had heard as a young child about the "mark of the beast." This placing of a Personal Identification Number on each person's body sounded an awful lot like what she had heard in those sermons.

Melinda had agreed to come for implantation only after John had pointed out that Pope Peter II had endorsed this program. Since the Pope himself was Christian, there surely couldn't be anything wrong with this new system. Plus, how would they feed their kids if they didn't get their validations?

The conversations taking place up and down the line were most interesting. One woman stated loudly, "My ex will never disappear with my kids again. Within fifteen minutes, the cops will nail his hide."

Another remarked, "This will be great for my business. We won't ever again have to worry about bad checks. Do you realize how much money we lose every month because of bad checks?"

Melinda noticed a man and woman up ahead of them. They didn't appear to be waiting for validation. Instead, they were working their way slowly through the line talking to people. She noticed that three or four people actually dropped out of line after talking to them for a while. *I wonder who they are and what they are doing?* She really couldn't tell for sure since they were being quite discreet.

Melinda returned to her conversation with John. "Will this chip implantation hurt?" she asked apprehensively.

"No," he replied. "The letter said it is totally painless. They've had this technology perfected for quite some time now. Melinda, just relax. You're getting on my nerves!"

Melinda noticed John's irritation. *I don't think he's as comfortable with this as he has tried to let on,* she worried.

151

About that time the couple who had been moving along the line, talking to different ones, slid in beside them. "Hi! We're Larry and Samantha Hightower," the man said. "We don't mean to intrude, but have you ever been told about a prophecy in the Bible that foretells a time when every person will be forced to have a number in order to buy or sell?"

John curtly replied, "Look, I've heard a lot of prophecies preached through the years that never did happen. I just don't put any stock in any of them. A lot of those prophecy preachers made a big deal about Y2K. And you know what happened with that—nothing! Look, I don't mean to be rude about all this, but we're a little edgy already."

Larry said reassuringly, "I know how you feel. Linda and I don't mean to upset you. Let me just show you exactly what the prophecy says. If the fact that a cashless system, just like the one you are getting ready to volunteer for, was described in the Bible two thousand years ago doesn't mean anything to you, we'll leave you alone. You know, we don't have anything to gain by being here. We just know that if you take this mark, you will be lost forever. Just look at what it says right here in Revelation 14:9-11: '...If any man worship the beast and his image, and receive his mark in his forehead, or in his hand, the same shall drink of the wine of the wrath of God, which is poured out without mixture into the cup of His indignation; and he shall be tormented with fire and brimstone in the presence of the holy angels, and in the presence of the Lamb: and the smoke of their torment ascendeth up for ever and ever: and they have no rest day nor night, who worship the beast and his image, and whosoever receiveth the mark of his name.' Folks, the decision you are making right now is a matter of eternal life or eternal death!"

Melinda broke in. "John, I don't want to go through with this number validation. I've been against it ever since we got the letter."

John shot back, "You want to eat, don't you? You want to feed your kids, don't you? Do you realize I'll lose my job if I don't take this mark?"

Melinda started to cry. "Please, John. Let's at least take a few days to think this over. I've heard all of my life that this was coming someday. Now here it is. Please, I don't want to do this. We can come back next week if we change our minds," she pleaded.

Larry stepped forward, "John, why don't you come to our house for a bite of lunch? We'll go through all the Scriptures about this and answer any questions that you and your wife have. That will at least give you some time to think."

"Well, okay," John finally agreed. "But I sure hate having to go through this twice."

Over lunch Larry went through the entire subject point by point. "Two thousand years ago, the prophecy was given that an economic system would be set up in which every person would use a number for buying and selling. This was prophesied before the invention of the computer or the Internet. Yet, it would be impossible for such a system to operate without these recent inventions! The prophecy states that this cashless economic system would be put in place at the same time that a system of global government was established on earth."

"All this business about the need for global government began at the fall of the Berlin Wall," John broke in. "I remember President Bush saying that the fall of the wall was the beginning of the New World Order."

"That's right," Larry said. "As a matter of fact, the Bible prophesied that the fall of the Berlin Wall would be the event that would trigger the formation of the one-world government."

"The Bible says that?" John questioned. "Wow! That's unbelievable."

Larry and Samantha talked with John and Melinda for the rest of the afternoon. By that evening, both John and Melinda were ready to give their lives to Jesus Christ, no matter the cost.

As Melinda slipped into bed that night, she whispered a prayer of thanksgiving to God for Larry and Samantha. She shuddered when she realized how close she and John had come to selling their souls to Antichrist Arachev. "Thank You, God," she prayed. "Thank You so much!"

At the courthouse that afternoon, Jack and Beverly House stepped into the validation room. They had rudely rejected Larry and Samantha's attempts to warn them of the irreversible consequences of what they were getting ready to do.

"Before we can implant your number, you are required to take the anti-terrorism pledge and the pledge of allegiance," the governmental agent said. "Jack, remove your hat. Both of you, place your hands over your hearts and face the screen where President Arachev is." When Jack and Beverly turned toward the screen, they saw Arachev standing with a UN flag just to his left. "Now repeat after me," the agent continued. "I pledge allegiance to the flag of the United Nations of the World, and to the global government for which it stands, one world, indivisible with peace and security for all. I pledge allegiance to the Global Ethic, I acknowledge that all religious beliefs have value and should be respected, and I promise not to incite religious conflict by attempting to proselytize other global citizens to my beliefs. And I believe Michael Arachev is God's anointed leader to bring peace and security to Mother Earth."

When the implantation was performed, Beverly hardly felt anything at all. Afterward, the Houses were given a booklet explaining exactly how to function in the new totally cashless society.

They decided to stop by the grocery store on the way home. They needed a few things, and besides, they were sort of anxious to try this new system out! They loaded the things they needed into sacks as they shopped. Then they merely placed the sacks into the grocery cart as the booklet had instructed. Once they had everything they needed, Jack headed for the exit. "Jack, what are you doing?!" Beverly protested.

"I'm going home," came Jack's mischievous reply.

"You can't do that," Beverly insisted. "You're going to get us arrested!"

As they passed through the last set of doors, a store employee called out, "Ma'am!" Beverly's heart sank.

She hissed at Jack, "Now what are we going to do?"

The employee came alongside of her. "You forgot your receipt," he said. By now Jack was doubled over with laughter.

"Do you mean that all these groceries were scanned right in our sacks?" The employee nodded. Beverly couldn't believe it!

"Our implanted number was automatically scanned too," Jack noted. "Everything is already paid for."

Wow! This is nice, Beverly thought as she followed Jack to the car. *I'm going to like this new system. No more grocery checkout lines for me.*

Jack always liked to watch the 11 o'clock news before going off to bed. That evening the broadcast was full of the new society's implementation of the validation chip. Pictures of the lines of people waiting in front of their courthouses appeared on the television. They actually showed one family being implanted to illustrate how painless it was. The one thing they didn't show was the required pledge of allegiance and the loyalty oath. Beverly wondered why they had avoided showing that.

The last item of news dealt with the religious radicals who were trying to sabotage the wonderful new cashless system. The television cameras caught on film some of the fundamentalist Christians who were moving up and down the line trying to scare people with their stupid prophecies.

Suddenly, a deep hatred welled up inside of Beverly toward these religious radicals. *Those are the kinds of people who cause tension and war on earth. They should put them all behind bars or get rid of them any way they can*, she thought. For a moment, the depth of her hatred toward these people whom she didn't even know somewhat surprised her. She had never felt such strong hatred toward anybody before. "What happened to me?" she wondered aloud. "Why, I wouldn't care if they marched every one of them off to the gas chambers!" Beverly knew this new attitude should alarm her, but it didn't. It seemed to her the right way to think. Had something happened to her when she had taken the loyalty oath to Michael Arachev? She

157

wasn't sure. All she knew was that the world could no longer tolerate these political and religious dissidents who insisted on holding onto their right-wing beliefs irregardless of the common good!

Much of that night, Beverly dreamed of bowing before the image of President Arachev. In her dreams, she felt overwhelming adoration for the world leader. Then she would dream of the radical Christians trying to witness to Jack and her. In her dreams, their witnessing made her so angry that she wanted to hurt them. President Arachev was the greatest political leader the world had ever seen, and he had come on the world scene at just the right time! Those stupid, redneck ingrates! Those radical Christians think they are the only ones who are right. They think everyone else is going to hell. It's people like that who have caused war, genocide, and the holocaust.

Beverly awoke the next morning in a very dark mood.

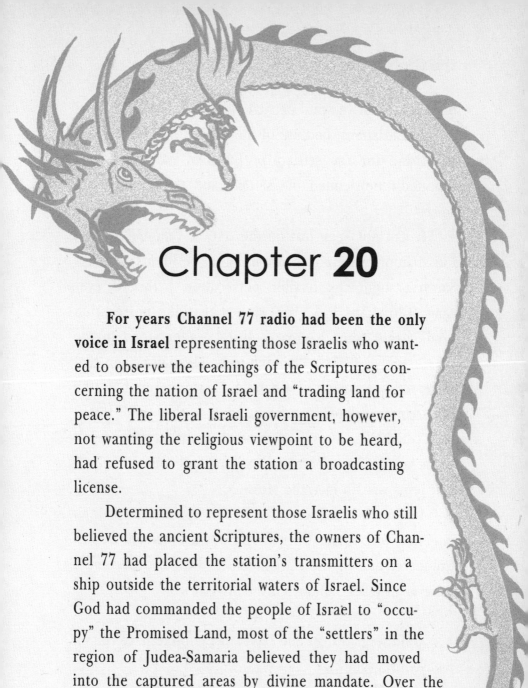

Chapter 20

For years Channel 77 radio had been the only voice in Israel representing those Israelis who wanted to observe the teachings of the Scriptures concerning the nation of Israel and "trading land for peace." The liberal Israeli government, however, not wanting the religious viewpoint to be heard, had refused to grant the station a broadcasting license.

Determined to represent those Israelis who still believed the ancient Scriptures, the owners of Channel 77 had placed the station's transmitters on a ship outside the territorial waters of Israel. Since God had commanded the people of Israel to "occupy" the Promised Land, most of the "settlers" in the region of Judea-Samaria believed they had moved into the captured areas by divine mandate. Over the years, Channel 77 had become the voice of the settlers.

At first the conservative station had been bitterly opposed to the Christian movement that was sweeping through Israel. In spite of vitriolic attacks from Channel 77, the Christians, because of their love for the nation of Israel and for the settlers of Judea in particular, had repeatedly befriended the settlers and their lone radio voice.

It had not been lost on the staff at Channel 77 that Christian organizations had warned the residents of Judea-Samaria about the terrible persecution before it ever came. Christians had even warned that the persecution would begin when a great political leader stood in the rebuilt Jewish Temple claiming to be Messiah. When that came to pass, many at Channel 77 wondered how the Christians had known so far in advance that these things were coming. As a result of these different factors, several of the key staff members at the station had come to believe that Jesus was, in fact, the Messiah.

It was a big step when the owners consented to air an interview with Roger Cornell and David Freeman. Dennis Goldberg, one of the staff members who had become a believer in Jesus, conducted the interview.

Goldberg: "Roger and David, it's good to have you on today's program."

Cornell: "Thank you so much for having us. We've been listeners of Channel 77 for many years."

Goldberg: "You have been preaching for several years now that a time of unprecedented persecution was coming for the residents of Judea. That time has now arrived. How did you come to know this?"

Cornell: "We knew this from some very specific prophecies in the Bible."

Goldberg: "Are you speaking of prophecies from the Torah?"

Cornell: "That point is what made this whole issue difficult to convey to the Jewish people. The prophecies were not from what we call the Old Testament. They were prophecies spoken by Jesus Himself as He sat on the Mount of Olives."

Goldberg: "I'll confess to you, I originally rejected what you were saying because the prophecies came from Jesus. But after several of the other prophecies that you taught happened, I felt I was forced to reevaluate."

Freeman: "Dennis, when was it that you began to take a second look?"

Goldberg: "The first big thing that happened was when our government began to give the areas of Judea-Samaria over to Palestinian control. I couldn't believe they were willing to surrender our Promised Land after God had so miraculously placed it in our hands. Yet you had said that the government would do that. At that time, I began to have a gnawing suspicion inside of me that there was something that I had missed."

Freeman: "What did you do then?"

Goldberg: "Nothing, really, at that time. I just began to wonder if the prophecies concerning horrible slaughter ahead for the inhabitants of Judea might not be right. It was when the announcement came concerning building the Third Temple north of the Dome of the Rock that you really captured my attention. As you know, those of us who respect God and His Word just couldn't believe that any Israeli would agree to leaving two pagan shrines on the mount where God promised to place His name. When our leaders consented to build the Third Temple right beside these pagan houses of worship, that was a big wake-up call for me! That's when I began to study the prophecies in earnest."

Cornell: "So, Dennis, when did you finally come to know that Jesus was, in fact, the Messiah?"

Goldberg: "It was obvious to me from the beginning that President Arachev was not a true friend to Israel, though many Israelis thought he was. When Arachev and Pope Peter II emerged as the political and spiritual leaders of the world, I knew the handwriting was on the wall. I was finally born again on the first night of your first prophecy conference in Jerusalem."

Cornell: "We realize it's a huge step for a Jewish person to accept the fact that Jesus is the Messiah. You face possible ostracism from your family, the loss of your job, and persecution by the entire religious sector of the Jewish community. I'm so thankful that God is now giving thousands like yourself the courage to stand for truth, no matter what the consequences are."

Goldberg: "Let's talk about what's going to happen next. There are so many listening today who are desperately in need of direction. Roger, according to the prophecies of the Bible, what does the road ahead hold for the nation of Israel and for the world in general?"

Cornell: "The next year or two will be the best of times and yet the worst of times. The Bible is explicit that we have now entered the time referred to as the Great Tribulation. Jesus said of this time, '...then shall be great tribulation, such as was not since the beginning of the world to this time, no, nor ever shall be.'"

Goldberg: "How long will this time of great tribulation last?"

Cornell: "From the time when Arachev stood in the temple claiming to be the Messiah until the end of the Great Tribulation, will be three and one-half years."

Goldberg: "You know, the shame is that Arachev seemed to have some good ideas when he first burst onto the world scene. We here in Israel absolutely loved him. How did all this go so wrong?"

Freeman: "Dennis, you know the old adage—'Power corrupts, and absolute power corrupts absolutely.' I think that is what has happened here. Besides, anything that is not based on the truth will ultimately fail. Arachev is presently repeating the same mistakes that Adolf Hitler made. Hitler began to see himself as having attained godlike status. That's where Arachev is right now. He has been so exalted by the world press and by Pope Peter II that he has come to see himself as the Messiah, even God."

Goldberg: "One of the most deceptive things about this entire global scheme is that everything is being done in the name of 'human rights.' We have never seen such a rapid loss of liberty, and it's all being propagated under the guise of protecting liberty. We can't speak against homosexuality, even if we know God clearly teaches against it, because of offending the gay community. Never mind that these people will be eternally lost if they continue in their present lifestyle. We are not supposed to try to convert anyone to Jesus since this could supposedly produce such religious strife that the peace of the New World Order would be disturbed. Thus we now have hate crime laws on the books against proselytizing. And we must pledge allegiance to Arachev himself and affirm our belief in the Global Ethic—all in the name of human rights. What an incredible deception!"

Cornell: "The alarming thing is that all this is going to get worse before it gets better. The same prophecies that told us of a numbering system that would be used to force compliance to the prophesied one-world government also tell us that many will ultimately be put to death who refuse to comply."

Goldberg: "It is so hard to believe that people could be put to death just because they refuse to change their religious beliefs and conform to those dictated by the government. It's really hard to believe this could happen in this age of enlightenment."

Cornell: "It's hard to believe until we remember that six million Jews were marched to gas chambers mere decades ago."

Goldberg: "Ouch! That's painful to even think about!"

Freeman: "It is hard to think about, but we must be thinking about it. We've done as well as we have under this oppressive economic system because we knew it was coming and took measures to circumvent it. The Bible tells us to be 'wise as serpents, and harmless as doves.' We need to be thinking ahead as to how we can avoid the persecutions yet to come."

Goldberg: "What should we be doing?"

Freeman: "First of all, what should we *not* be doing? We should not be stockpiling weapons. Jesus taught us that '...all they that take the sword shall perish with the sword.' If we can avoid the coming persecutions, we should take measures to do so. Even Jesus avoided attempts on His life when He knew it wasn't yet time for Him to die. Furthermore, we have to realize that some are going to be put to death. If that becomes unavoidable, then we should not fear. We know that death is only the doorway that leads to eternal life with Jesus."

Goldberg: "I regret to say that we are out of time for this segment of our program. Roger Cornell and David

Freeman, it has been a pleasure and an honor to have you on Channel 77. Thank you so much."

That night one of the planes of Arachev's World Community dropped a bomb on the ship housing the transmitters of Channel 77. Within ten minutes the ship had listed badly to the south, then slid slowly under the chilly waters of the Mediterranean.

Chapter **21**

What was it about this city that attracted every would-be world emperor like a moth to the flame? Somehow, they could not resist. Give them the whole world, and still they had to have Jerusalem. They risked everything they possessed in order to control this place. Michael Arachev was no exception.

Jerusalem was the one issue that blocked a final resolution to the conflict between Israelis and Palestinians. The two sides simply could not agree. The Palestinians wanted to at least control East Jerusalem. Israel was unwilling to surrender control of any of the Holy City. In order to cool things down, determining the final status of Jerusalem was put off for a while. What neither side knew was that Arachev wanted it for himself. He agreed to postpone a final compromise so that he could figure out a way to claim it himself.

Arachev had never forgotten the way he felt when he stood in the Temple and said those words, "I am your Messiah." Something powerful had surged through him that day. From then on it seemed his powers of insight and oratory were heightened. Sometimes the most brilliant ideas would present themselves to him seemingly from nowhere. At other times dark brooding moods would settle over him. Never before had he experienced the levels of intellectual enlightenment and the depths of depression that swept over him since that fateful day.

The Palestinians are the key, Arachev thought to himself. *They are never happy. They will not be happy until every Jew is driven from the land of Israel. They claim they care about Jerusalem, but they turn their backs on it when they pray. They don't care about Jerusalem. They just don't want the Jews to have it.*

Herein lay Arachev's secret plan. If the Jerusalem issue could be agitated until the World Community demanded that it be settled, then his time would have come. Once tensions became so great that armed conflict appeared to be inevitable, then the World Community would demand action.

From the beginning, the United Nations had wanted Jerusalem for itself. Every world leader knows that Jerusalem is the crown jewel of the earth. When Palestine was partitioned by the United Nations in 1947, Jerusalem was declared an international city under UN control. From then until the present, the World Community has never recognized Jerusalem as Israel's capital. *Yes, sooner or later*

I will have Jerusalem, Arachev thought. *The only question is when.*

Opportunity came knocking sooner than he thought possible. About three years after the temple dedication, Palestinian Secretary of State Mohammed Bassad brought the subject up. "When are we going to resolve the outstanding issues concerning Jerusalem?" he asked. "You asked us to be patient, and I think we have been about as patient as you could expect anyone to be. You know those Israelis. They could stall forever. You and I both know that International Law says that all territories taken in war must be returned. East Jerusalem was taken in the 1967 War. Are we going to enforce International Law, or not?"

"You know how set the Israelis are on this issue," Arachev reasoned. "Logic doesn't work with them when it comes to Jerusalem. Of course, you have a point. International Law must be enforced. But it will be much easier when Israel's disarmament is complete."

Exasperated, Bassad spoke through clenched teeth, "You know the Israelis won't be disarmed twenty-five years from now. The international community didn't wait for the disarmament of Yugoslavia before going to the aid of the Kosovars. But, of course, Israel always gets special treatment," Bassad added sarcastically.

The lid was off, and the genie was not going back into the bottle! The next Monday Mohammed Bassad presented a resolution to the UN Security Council demanding the total withdrawal of Israeli forces to pre-1967 borders. Immediately, world tensions escalated sharply.

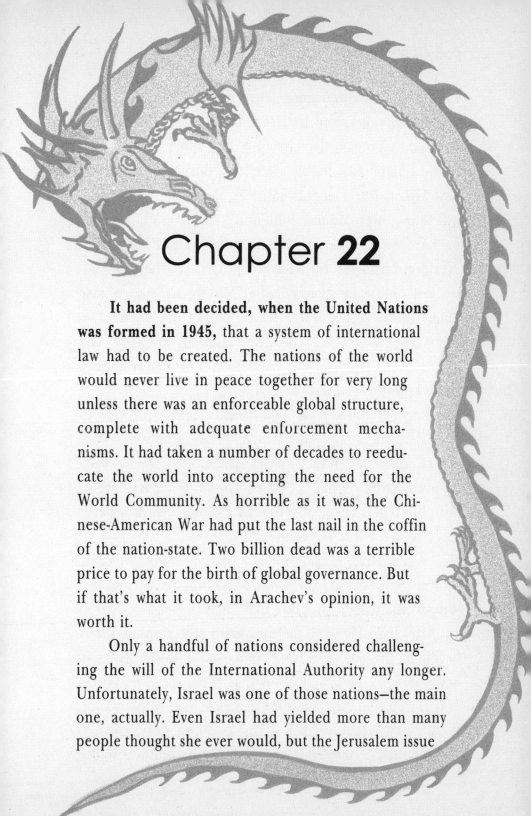

Chapter **22**

It had been decided, when the United Nations was formed in 1945, that a system of international law had to be created. The nations of the world would never live in peace together for very long unless there was an enforceable global structure, complete with adequate enforcement mechanisms. It had taken a number of decades to reeducate the world into accepting the need for the World Community. As horrible as it was, the Chinese-American War had put the last nail in the coffin of the nation-state. Two billion dead was a terrible price to pay for the birth of global governance. But if that's what it took, in Arachev's opinion, it was worth it.

Only a handful of nations considered challenging the will of the International Authority any longer. Unfortunately, Israel was one of those nations—the main one, actually. Even Israel had yielded more than many people thought she ever would, but the Jerusalem issue was considered untouchable. However, Arachev wasn't getting any younger, and he felt that the time had come to bring the arrogant Israelis into full submission to the World Community. Surely after Iraq, Bosnia, Kosovo, and East Timor, Israel would realize it was futile to resist the will of the international community.

Arachev smiled to himself. "We avoid the terms 'world government' or 'New World Order.' They are considered politically unacceptable. Yet we use the phrase 'international community,' which means the exact same thing, and no one so much as raises an eyebrow! The power to manipulate the masses with words is indeed remarkable," he mused.

Michael Arachev, through his emissaries, sent word to the Palestinians and to the Israelis of his intention to convene a new round of talks on Jerusalem. The Israelis reacted predictably: "What is this all about? What is there to talk about? Jerusalem is our eternal capital. We will never share it! We will never divide it!"

When Israel's ambassador, Simon Rosenthal, came calling the next day, the atmosphere was tense. But this was just the type of situation that Michael Arachev thrived on. After listening to all the time-worn objections, Arachev began to present his case. "Ambassador Rosenthal, you know how dangerous the world is these days. In World War I, we killed eight million. In World War II, 52 million died. Need I remind you of the 2 billion who perished in the Chinese-American war? We simply cannot tolerate war ever again. That's the reason I initiated these negotiations."

"But Chairman Arachev, Jerusalem is not a threat to world peace," Rosenthal argued.

"That's where you are wrong," Arachev said. "Jerusalem is the world's foremost threat to peace. You must understand that the only hope for lasting peace on earth is respect for international law. You know that international resolutions concerning the status of Jerusalem have been ignored since 1948. The whole world knows that Israel has thumbed its nose at global authority since 1967. The time has come for the World Community to insist on total compliance by every state on the face of the earth. Really, Ambassador Rosenthal, we have no choice. If there is going to be peace on earth, Jerusalem must be restored to the international status called for by UN Resolution 181.

"And why not?" Arachev continued persuasively. "Israelis will still be able to live there. Palestinians can live there. And yet everything will be administered fairly by the World Community."

"Mr. Chairman, you know that these terms will not be acceptable to my government!" Rosenthal protested hotly.

The reply was so predictable. "I'm afraid that you have no choice. Besides, this is a wonderful opportunity for Jerusalem to truly be the city of peace for all the world," Arachev suavely reasoned.

As Rosenthal left Arachev's palatial estate, he had a horrible, sickened feeling deep in the pit of his stomach. He remembered the words of Foreign Minister Ariel Sharon spoken behind closed doors during the NATO bombing of Yugoslavia. "Bosnia yesterday, Kosovo today, Jerusalem tomorrow."

Those words could end up being prophetic! Rosenthal thought.

The war of words heated up quickly. Pro-Israeli columnists and newscasters threw every argument they had into the battle.

"Jerusalem has never been any other nation's capital."

"Jerusalem is the only capital Israel has ever had for the past three thousand years."

"UN Resolution 181, which mandated that Jerusalem be an international entity, was rejected by the Arabs when they launched the war against Israel in 1948. Consequently, why should they now insist on its enforcement just because they lost the war that they themselves started?"

However, the globalist media ground away day after day. "The only hope for world peace is respect for international law. International law says that Jerusalem must be an international city under UN authority."

When public opinion was sufficiently mobilized, the resolution was presented to the UN Security Council. "The UN Security Council hereby demands that the City of Jerusalem be placed under UN authority as mandated by Resolution 181. Israel must withdraw her forces by

September 20th, allowing 20 thousand international peacekeeping troops to enter the city in order to enforce the rights of all people within the municipality of Jerusalem." The resolution passed the Security Council by a vote of 14 to 1. In previous years, the resolution would never have been approved since the United States had veto power. However, with the abolition of the veto on the Security Council, Israel was now at the mercy of the World Community.

Chapter 23

When Ambassador Rosenthal met with Israel's new prime minister, Yigal Alon, the next day, the discussion was grim. "Do you understand what this means, Mr. Ambassador?" Prime Minister Alon asked. "This means war! War against the World Community. Sharon was right when he said 'Bosnia yesterday, Kosovo today, and Jerusalem tomorrow.'"

"My thoughts exactly, Mr. Prime Minister," Rosenthal sighed.

The war of words in the media raged on for the next several weeks. Israel tried every diplomatic maneuver in her arsenal, but nothing worked. The one-world government trap was closing. Even while Israel desperately attempted to find a way out of the impending crisis, she feverishly prepared for war. Money was pumped into the military at an unprecedented rate. Military preparedness was heightened beyond any level previously experienced.

Israel's cabinet met continually during this time of crisis. Several of the members suggested that Israel should consider bowing to the demands of the World Community. "You don't think we can fight against the entire international community, do you?" they demanded.

Prime Minister Alon looked steadily at them. "Have any of you ever heard of David and Goliath? And besides, do you really think we will be allowed to live in peace if we capitulate on Jerusalem? You know the pent-up anti-Semitism that dominates the UN. The only thing that stopped them from moving against us before now was the U.S. veto. You know what the anti-Israeli votes in the UN General Assembly were as well as I do—149 to 1, 130 to 2, 150 to 1, and on and on."

"But resisting the World Community is insanity!" Shamir Mordechai protested. "This will mean the destruction of the State of Israel."

"Gentlemen, I think you have forgotten one thing. We still have the Samson Option," Alon stated flatly.

Mordechai couldn't believe his ears. They were sitting here discussing the use of nuclear weapons against the world government armies. Talk about national insanity! Yet, he could tell that Alon was dead serious.

Israel had convinced the French to sell the nuclear reactor to her in 1959. The facility had been constructed at Dimona in the Negev Desert. Israel had never admitted that she had nuclear weapons, but it was a well-known fact. *Jane's Intelligence Report* stated that satellites had spotted

two hundred nuclear installations in the area of Judea surrounding Jerusalem. The only thing the Israeli government had ever said was, "If we do have nuclear weapons,
we will never use them offensively. We will use them only
if our survival is at stake." Thus the name the "Samson
Option" was born. Simply stated, Israel was declaring to
the world, "If we go down, we're taking the house down
with us."

As the September 20th deadline drew near, global
tensions grew to frightening levels. Would the United
States intervene? Since losing 20 million of its citizens in
the conflict with China, very strong anti-war sentiments
had gained control in the U.S. Yet, there was still very
powerful support for the nation of Israel in America.

Russia was busy assembling a coalition to carry out
the operation against Israel. She had waited a long time
for the chance to move militarily against the Zionist entity. Iran, Libya, Ethiopia, and Turkey eagerly volunteered
for the campaign.

Russia said to the U.S., "We stood aside while you
whipped our buddy Saddam Hussein into line. Now we
expect you to stand by while we bring Israel under the control of the World Community." The word was that the U.S.

had promised to stay out of the conflict as long as the operation was kept within certain parameters.

The International Forces had never taken on as formidable a foe as Israel promised to be. The whole world knew that Israel's air force was the finest in the world. How do you move massive forces the required distances from Russia, through Syria, and then into Israel while coming under the withering air attack that Israel promised to administer? Add to that the need to bring the required heavy military equipment across the Euphrates River. There was no doubt that Israel would eliminate all the bridges that crossed the Euphrates. With that in mind, how do you manage to get tanks, half-tracks, and all the required vehicles across? It was a nightmare of a military logistic problem. But the die was cast, and the plans went forward.

Chairman Arachev was known for his deceit, but he was not one to hedge on a date, once he had delivered an ultimatum. By mid-September, troops began amassing in areas east of the Euphrates. Russia had installed very sophisticated anti-aircraft batteries throughout Syria. The level of fire they would be able to send against the invading Israeli bombers promised to be devastating.

Israel knew that the assault could come anytime after September 20th. They had activated all of their forces. The entire nation was like a coiled spring.

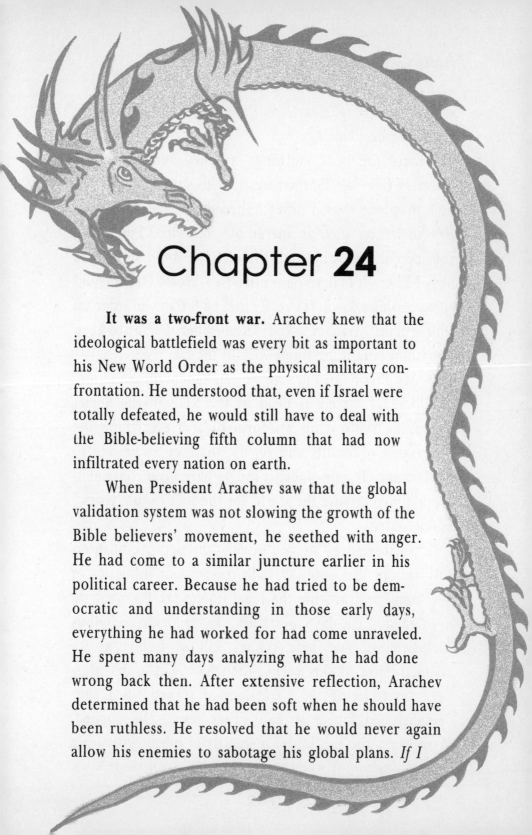

Chapter 24

It was a two-front war. Arachev knew that the ideological battlefield was every bit as important to his New World Order as the physical military confrontation. He understood that, even if Israel were totally defeated, he would still have to deal with the Bible-believing fifth column that had now infiltrated every nation on earth.

When President Arachev saw that the global validation system was not slowing the growth of the Bible believers' movement, he seethed with anger. He had come to a similar juncture earlier in his political career. Because he had tried to be democratic and understanding in those early days, everything he had worked for had come unraveled. He spent many days analyzing what he had done wrong back then. After extensive reflection, Arachev determined that he had been soft when he should have been ruthless. He resolved that he would never again allow his enemies to sabotage his global plans. *If I don't stop these religious fanatics now, I won't get another chance*, he decided.

Early the next morning, Arachev summoned his Attorney General. "Suslov, we have to squash these end-time prophecy nuts. I never believed that they would be able to muster such an incredible following. I'm telling you, people will believe anything! If we don't stop them now, I honestly believe our entire New World Order could come crashing down. It's really that bad! Can you come up with a plan?" Arachev asked. "Remember, I want to keep everything within the framework of the law."

"Mr. President, I'm sure we can handle this situation. Back when I served as head of the KGB in the Soviet Union, we made it an art form to give everything the appearance of legality and yet do whatever we needed to do. Fortunately, our globalist judges have been consistently appointed around the world for the past twenty years," Suslov stated.

"Furthermore," he continued, "the network of international law that you had such tremendous influence in developing will provide the legal framework for what we need to do. The laws pertaining to genocide, religious exclusiveness, and hate crimes will work just as we planned. Most of the world didn't have a clue that they were surrendering their freedom of speech when they demonstrated for those hate crime laws." He laughed. "You know, the media did a wonderful job of obscuring our real intentions when we were lobbying for those laws.

We weren't really wanting to punish the commission of the crime; we already had laws for that. We wanted to create a new system of laws that could punish people for what they thought and believed. And they bought it. Once we were able to get society used to the idea of punishing people for hate speech and hate beliefs, the way was prepared for the Global Ethic. Mr. President, we have all the legal basis that we need to deal with these Endtimers."

Arachev's set jaw showed his self-satisfaction. He would allow absolutely nothing to throw this world back into nationalism with all of its attendant evils. He was determined to bring closure both to his political opponents and to his religious opposition. He didn't merely want to destroy all political opposition, though. He also intended to stamp out the remaining religious cults that refused to bow the knee to his Global Ethic. Until political and religious unity was achieved, there would never really be peace on earth. Arachev knew that he was right, and he would not let some ignorant religious extremists thwart his benevolent plans for mankind now!

Plans were laid carefully for the sting operation that Arachev hoped would break the back of the Endtimers. The biggest problem was that there were so many of them.

There was no way that the millions of Bible believers could all be hauled off to jail. Consequently, they targeted the leaders of the movement.

The raids were scheduled for the middle of the night. This was designed to produce the maximum amount of terror. Women and children would be rudely awakened from their beds and men roughly dragged off to jail. False charges were filed against the Bible believers beforehand. They would be accused of planning terrorist attacks and acts of violence designed to trigger Armageddon.

Suslov planned to personally preside over the middle-of-the-night raids. (When he did, he was surprised at the Christians' lack of fear. Many of them actually would share the gospel with the very soldiers who were arresting them!)

But the most important mission of all was to arrest Roger Cornell and David Freeman. Both men had been working and preaching in the city of Jerusalem for the past several weeks. Between the radio, the Internet, and the huge prophecy conferences that were so popular, Roger and David were literally converting thousands to true biblical Christianity.

Arachev knew the importance of leadership. America had never fully recovered from the assassination of John F. Kennedy. Israel had not been able to rebound from the death of Yitzhak Rabin. Roger Cornell and David Freeman were strong leaders who had to be silenced at any cost!

Attorney General Suslov had chosen his most trusted lieutenants for this special part of the assignment. World Police Unit #2, headed by Sean Conkle from Scotland, was known for its efficiency and ruthlessness. This unit was sent to arrest Cornell. World Police Unit #17, under the command of Jacques Solano, was assigned to the arrest of Freeman. Solano had earned highest marks for his service during the World Community's actions against Bosnia and Kosovo. Suslov was certain that this operation would go off without a hitch. He had carefully crossed all the t's and dotted all the i's.

Even though Arachev and his henchmen continually accused the Bible believers of organizing secret militias and fomenting plans to overthrow the government, Suslov knew that none of this was true. He had personally listened to many hours of tapes produced by Cornell and Freeman. They clearly taught their followers to avoid armed conflict and violence. They stated repeatedly that Jesus and His disciples did not resist evil, and, therefore, 21st Century Christians should not fight either.

Knowing all this, Suslov felt almost ashamed to send such overwhelming force against the Christian leaders. He did not anticipate any resistance at all. But he knew that Arachev was absolutely seething with anger toward Cornell and Freeman. The articles they wrote and the sermons they gave were ripping Arachev's program for the World Community to shreds. It was as though they knew what Arachev was going to do before he ever did it. Suslov had actually begun to wonder if these two religious leaders weren't psychics or something. It was uncanny! He knew that President Arachev didn't merely want the leaders of the Endtimers movement stopped. He wanted them crushed!

Everything was set. At 2 a.m., the raids were to be launched. One of the first houses attacked was the residence of Dennis Goldberg. The loud banging at the door awakened Dennis out of his deep sleep. "Who is that?" his beautiful wife Hannah asked.

"I don't know," Dennis replied. "But it must be urgent. They sure are loud for the middle of the night."

As Dennis headed for the front door, apprehension began to engulf Hannah. "Was this it?" she wondered. They knew that sooner or later the crunch was going to come. Because of Dennis' role at Channel 77, they knew he could very well be a target. Hannah quickly moved to the window. She recognized the Global Police cars at the front curb. In spite of the tension of the moment, she couldn't help but notice the UN emblem on the side of each vehicle—the globe with the two olive branches around it. *The only peace that those olive branches stood for was the peace of subjugation and slavery,* she thought. The Marxists had always claimed to be for peace, too, as long as it was on their terms. Hannah quickly slipped into her robe. She knew right then that it was going to be a long night.

A couple of minutes later the International Police burst through the door of her bedroom. "Are you Hannah Goldberg?" they demanded.

"Yes," Hannah replied.

"Where do you work?" the officer in charge asked accusingly.

"I don't hold a public job, sir," Hannah answered. "I raise my family while my husband makes the living."

"Where are your children?" the officer demanded. He went barging back out into the hallway and into the small bedroom where Zach and Rachel were asleep.

Rachel, startled by being awakened by a stranger in the middle of the night, cried out, "Mommy!"

Hannah rushed past the peacekeepers and sat on the bed beside Rachel. "It's all right, baby," she assured her. "It's going to be all right."

"Who are these men, Mommy?" Rachel asked. "What are they doing here?"

Peacekeeper Wilhelm looked at Hannah. He said, "We'll take care of the children now."

Hannah didn't move. "Officer, do you have any children?" she asked.

"Yes, I have three," came the reply. "But I'm not raising them to be religious extremists who will someday grow up to be a threat to world peace." The reply was harsh, but Hannah thought she noticed a softening in his demeanor.

About that time, Dennis stepped into the room. "Officer, Hannah and the children have done nothing. Arrest me if you must, but please let Hannah stay here with the children." Dennis' request was neither defiant nor disrespectful.

It was at that moment that Rachel chimed in, "Please, officer, you know how much children need their mommies. Let Mommy stay with us. Please?"

It was a request that even Officer Wilhelm could not resist. "Mrs. Goldberg, don't call anyone. Don't cause any trouble. If you create any disturbance at all, I will be forced to come back for you and take the children to the reeducation center."

"Thank you, officer. Thank you very much."

Hannah watched out the bedroom window as the peacekeepers shoved Dennis into a Global Police car. She noticed several of their neighbors watching from their windows as well. But she was not ashamed. As a matter of fact, she was very proud of her husband. What a wonderful man he was! He had shown no fear through the entire ordeal, and he had conducted himself like the true Christian that he was.

Hannah turned to her children who watched her from their beds. Zach asked, "Mommy, what are they going to do to Daddy? Why did they take him away?"

Hannah spoke with the assurance of one who has total faith in God. "Everything is going to be all right. They want to ask him some questions. God will take care of everything."

"But why did they come in the middle of the night, Mommy?" the older, more perceptive Rachel inquired.

"Well, they don't like it because we are Christians. They got us out of bed like this because they are trying to scare us into denying Jesus as our Lord," Hannah explained.

Rachel sat straight up and said bravely, "But that will never work with us, will it? We love Jesus before anything— even life itself, huh?" Hannah was so glad for those daily devotions when she and Dennis had taught their children absolute loyalty to Jesus, no matter what happened. They had known this moment would probably come.

Well, test number one was passed with flying colors...at least by the children, Hannah thought.

Finally, after a long while, Zach and Rachel drifted off to sleep. Hannah was left alone. "It would be nice to talk to a fellow Christian right now," she sighed quietly. But she didn't dare make that phone call. She had no doubt that every form of communication in and out of their house was being monitored—well, except for one. Alone in her bedroom, she slipped to her knees. "Jesus, You said that we would be hated of all nations for Your name's sake. I guess that prophecy has to come to pass, too. Lord, be with Dennis. Give him strength to stand.

Even if they threaten to harm the children and me, please help him not to give in."

Hannah and Dennis had discussed this possibility many times. As they saw the prophecies being fulfilled, they had talked about what they might face. Hannah had lectured Dennis over and over, "Even if they threaten to hurt me and the children in front of you, you must not deny Jesus as your Lord. I know it would be terrible for you, Dennis. But we are in this together. Anything that they could do to us here, no matter how terrible, is only temporary. We must always remember what Jesus said: 'Fear none of those things which thou shalt suffer: behold, the devil shall cast some of you into prison, that ye may be tried...be thou faithful unto death, and I will give thee a crown of life.'"

Hannah got up from her knees with the assurance that God's wonderful presence was with Dennis in the jail cell at that very moment. "Thank You, Lord," she whispered. "I love You."

The Global Police had been tailing Roger Cornell and David Freeman for days in preparation for the anticipated raid. The report came back that Cornell and Freeman usually slept in different houses and moved around a lot.

Their behavior was typical for persons who were attempting to avoid arrest or maybe even assassination.

Suslov digested this interesting piece of news carefully. *They suspect that something is up,* he thought. *How do they always seem to know?* he wondered. Suslov did not want to botch this arrest. He had seen Arachev when he was angry, and it was not a pretty sight. The man did not suffer fools lightly. Suslov ordered that both Cornell and Freeman be kept under surveillance right up to the time of the arrest.

Jean Sirstad sat in his blue sedan across from the home of Eli and Naomi Levi, the place Cornell was staying that night. Because the car windows were tinted so darkly, Sirstad was virtually invisible. He watched as Cornell went into the house at around 8 o'clock. Sirstad observed carefully as lights were either turned on or off in each room. Central Police Headquarters had provided him with a diagram of the entire house. Of course, the layout of every house under Arachev's dominion was filed on the central computer of the World Community.

At about 11 o'clock, lights came on in one of the bedrooms. His intelligence report showed that Cornell usually went to bed around eleven. Sirstad noted which room it was. The commander of the raiding unit would want to know. By 11:30, all the lights in the house were out.

Sirstad sent his report back to headquarters. "Officer Jean Sirstad reporting to Global Headquarters. Suspect Roger Cornell entered the residence of Naomi and Eli Levi located at 3310 Rothschild Avenue at approximately

8 p.m. No one was observed leaving the house after that time. At 11 p.m., lights came on in the room in which Cornell is believed to be sleeping. By 11:30 p.m., all lights in the home were off. It seems certain that Cornell has now retired for the night."

Acknowledgement came over Sirstad's police radio. "Affirmative. Operation is proceeding as planned. Maintain surveillance until operation is completed. If any changes occur, please advise. Over."

Jean Sirstad was the top surveillance specialist in the entire Global Police force. He did not have one blemish on his record. He had never been known to mishandle an assignment.

Sirstad glanced at his watch. Twelve o'clock. It had been a long day. His eyes tried to go shut, but he steeled himself against the intruding drowsiness. Many years of training had taught him how to ward off the urge to sleep that could become so overpowering about this time of the night. He had never fallen asleep while on assignment. He just wouldn't allow himself to do it!

He noticed a porch light come on four houses down on the opposite side of the street. Immediately, he was totally alert. Then he saw the small poodle slip outside and the robed woman waiting at the door. In less than two minutes, the dog was back inside, and the light was off. Obviously, nothing was going on there.

Sirstad looked one more time at the Levi residence. Dark. He closed his eyes to rest them for just a moment.

Oblivion swept over him. After a while, his eyes came back open. Startled, he sat up. He couldn't believe it! He had fallen asleep! In a panic he looked at his watch—12:45. He had been asleep for almost 45 minutes! He had never done that before! What in the world had come over him?

Nearly in panic, Sirstad's eyes scanned the house carefully. Nothing was changed. The lights were still off. No movement showed anywhere. *That was close*, he thought.

He was startled by the crackling of the radio. "Attention, Officer 45763." (That was his Personal Identification Number.) "Any changes observed at your post of surveillance?"

Sirstad quickly replied, "None, sir." He felt pangs of guilt at not reporting his problem with drowsiness. But he had an unblemished record, and he wasn't about to let it be ruined by a brief nap while watching a preacher in bed. He was sure nothing had happened, anyway.

At 1:55 a.m., an unmarked Global Police car cruised quietly past. *The operation is on!* Sirstad thought. He knew that soon the street would be blocked and the Levi house surrounded.

At exactly 2 a.m., 15 Global Police cars converged on the Levi residence. Sirstad was shocked to see Attorney General Suslov in the lead car. *There must be more to this than anyone has said*, he concluded. He was used to being in on highly important operations, but the Attorney General...?

Quickly, officers surrounded the house. Four guard-
ed the back door, while two were stationed under each
window. Six Global Police officers made their way to the
front. Sirstad could hear the loud knock clear out at his
car. Right away, lights began to come on in the Levi house.
The first lights were in the room belonging to Naomi and
Eli Levi. Then the hall lights. The officer knocked again—
this time louder. Then the living room lights were
switched on.

Sirstad watched. "Why hasn't Cornell turned his light
on? He's got to be awake by now," he muttered. A tight
knot of fear began to form in the pit of Sirstad's stomach.
"Calm down," he said to himself. "You're letting your
imagination run away with you!"

The officer demanded to see Roger Cornell. Eli Levi
tried to stall. "Is something wrong, officer?" Levi asked.
"It's most unusual to come barging into the house of an
Israeli citizen at two in the morning."

"Get Cornell this minute, or my officers will turn this
house upside down," Sean Conkle demanded. Levi knew
this was no idle threat.

"Okay, okay. I'll get him. Just a moment." Eli walked
down the hallway to the door of the front bedroom.
"Roger," he called. No answer. He knocked on the door
loudly. "Roger, the police are here demanding to see you."
No answer. Conkle stepped to the end of the hallway so
that he could observe what was going on. Eli turned to
him. "He's not answering, sir."

"Then you go in and wake him up," Conkle ordered. "Hurry up. We have a schedule to keep." Eli turned the knob, but it was locked.

"Officer, something must be wrong. He's obviously in there, but he's not answering," Eli said worriedly. "Perhaps he has become ill. I'll get the room key."

When Eli opened the door and turned on the light, he was as surprised at what he saw as Officer Conkle was. The bed was empty! "What is this?!" Conkle shouted. He grabbed Eli around the neck. "Tell me this minute where he is," he demanded, "or I'll put you behind bars, and you'll never come out. We have ways of making people like you talk!"

"Officer, I don't know where Roger is," Eli protested. "A little before 11 o'clock I told him good night. Then he came into this room. I don't know what has happened to him."

Conkle paused. *Either this guy is one incredible actor, or he is telling me the truth.* He had learned in earlier dealings with these Bible believers that they would not lie to you—even if their lives were in danger.

Now what? Conkle wondered. He didn't intend to go back empty-handed. Turning to his officers, he ordered, "Search this house. Don't miss one potential hiding place. I mean it! If you guys don't know it, the orders for Cornell's arrest came straight from President Arachev!" This interesting piece of information was not lost on Eli Levi.

For the next two hours, Conkle's men took the Levi house apart. Officers ended up in the attic, the crawl space under the floor—everywhere. They found nothing.

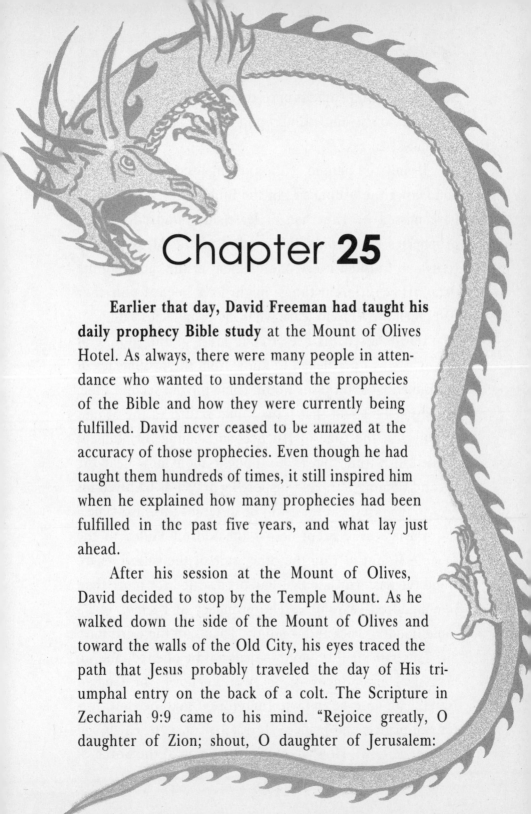

Chapter 25

Earlier that day, David Freeman had taught his daily prophecy Bible study at the Mount of Olives Hotel. As always, there were many people in attendance who wanted to understand the prophecies of the Bible and how they were currently being fulfilled. David never ceased to be amazed at the accuracy of those prophecies. Even though he had taught them hundreds of times, it still inspired him when he explained how many prophecies had been fulfilled in the past five years, and what lay just ahead.

After his session at the Mount of Olives, David decided to stop by the Temple Mount. As he walked down the side of the Mount of Olives and toward the walls of the Old City, his eyes traced the path that Jesus probably traveled the day of His triumphal entry on the back of a colt. The Scripture in Zechariah 9:9 came to his mind. "Rejoice greatly, O daughter of Zion; shout, O daughter of Jerusalem:

behold, thy King cometh unto thee: He is just, and having salvation; lowly, and riding upon an ass, and upon a colt the foal of an ass."

If only the people at the time of Jesus' First Coming had known the prophecies of the Bible! They would never have missed it. They had at least one hundred specific prophecies concerning the coming of the Messiah, and Jesus had fulfilled every one of them in the most minute detail. How different things might have been if only they had taken the time to learn what the prophecies said.

David raised his eyes to the crest of the Mount of Olives. He was privileged to know from the prophecies of the Bible that soon Jesus would come for the second time. Zechariah 14:4 said that Jesus would return to the Mount of Olives at the time of His Second Coming. Excitement swelled up within him as he thought about how near the Second Coming was. He whispered a prayer as he lifted his eyes to the skies, "Lord, it will be different this next time."

David's eyes swept across the Kidron Valley to the Temple Mount just on the other side of the valley. There stood the Eastern Gate that had been sealed for more than four hundred years now. The prophecy of Ezekiel 44:2-3 came flooding back to his mind: "Then said the Lord unto me; This gate shall be shut, it shall not be opened, and no man shall enter in by it; because the Lord, the God of Israel, hath entered in by it, therefore it shall be shut. It is for the prince; the prince, He shall sit in it to eat bread before the Lord; He shall enter by the way of the porch of that gate, and shall go out by the way of the same." The sealed gate actually looked like a bride in waiting...simply standing silently until its appointment with destiny. These thoughts made the return of Jesus seem so near and filled David with awe.

As he continued on toward the Western Wall Plaza, a person he didn't know slipped up beside him. "Hi. My name is Uri. Aren't you one of those two preachers who speak on the prophecies of the Bible and how close we are to the coming of Messiah?"

"Yes. My name is David—David Freeman."

"I like a lot of what you say. But could I ask you a question?" Uri inquired.

"Sure. Ask anything that you want. I'll answer you if I can," David assured.

"You're a Christian, right?"

"Yes." David knew what was coming next.

Uri continued, "How could you expect us Jews to believe in Jesus when so many Christians have persecuted us and put us to death? Did you know that Adolf Hitler thought he was doing the work of God when he tried to annihilate the Jewish race?"

David chose his words very carefully. "Uri, the people who did those horrible things to your people were not Christians, even though they claimed to be. They were false Christians. A true Christian would not hurt anyone, let alone God's chosen people on this earth. You gave us our Messiah, and every single word of our Bible was recorded by your people. I know that this point is a tremendous stumbling block to Jewish people when they begin to consider that perhaps Jesus was their Messiah. The simple truth is that anyone who would persecute the Jewish people is not a Christian, no matter what they claim."

"I like what you and Roger say, but I still have this deep distrust of Christians. It has been drilled into me all of my life," Uri said pensively.

"I understand, Uri. I can't say that I blame you. But consider this—would Roger and I be here in Israel preaching if we didn't have a genuine love for you and your people? Every day that we are here, we are risking our lives. Someday Arachev and his henchmen will kill us. But, by God's help, we will continue to teach the truth until that time comes."

"What you say makes a lot of sense to me," Uri admitted. "How can I know for certain that Jesus was the Messiah?"

"Uri, let's quickly list the prophecies that foretold what Messiah would do when He came. Then let's see if Jesus fulfilled those prophecies.

"We'll keep it simple," David continued. "Messiah was to be from the tribe of Judah. Was Jesus from the tribe of Judah? Yes.

"His birthplace had to be in Bethlehem. Was Jesus born in Bethlehem? Yes.

"And He would be rejected as the Messiah, according to Isaiah 53:3. Is He rejected?"

Uri broke in, "I see it now! I've been guilty of fulfilling that prophecy. I've rejected Jesus all of my life."

"Yes, Uri," David continued, "and this same passage in Isaiah 53 says that the Messiah would be wounded for our transgressions."

"David, I never expected a Messiah who would be wounded for my sins. I've always looked for a political leader."

"Like Arachev?" David asked.

"Yes! Exactly!" Uri said in amazement. "Wow, I didn't realize how misguided I've been."

David continued, "The prophecies also say that the Messiah would ride into Jerusalem on the foal of an ass, which Jesus did.

"They say He would be betrayed by a trusted friend. Judas, one of Jesus' twelve disciples, betrayed Him.

"Zechariah 11:12 foretold that the price of betrayal would be thirty pieces of silver. That's the exact amount that the priests gave to Judas for his part in the conspiracy."

Uri couldn't believe it. "Are you saying that the exact amount of the betrayal money was prophesied in the Book of Zechariah five hundred years before it happened? That's incredible! Why wouldn't anybody believe that?"

"You tell me, Uri," David said. "Why haven't you believed it?"

"Because I didn't know that was in Zechariah," Uri answered.

"Exactly," came David's reply. "That's the reason Roger and I are doing what we are doing. That's the reason for the radio interviews, the prophecy conferences, all the videos, tapes, and literature."

"David, I see it!" Uri shouted. "It is so clear that Jesus came as our Messiah, but we missed Him because we didn't know the Scriptures. What do I need to do?"

David said, "I'll need to sit down with you and explain the gospel. Are you free later this evening?"

"This evening will be fine," Uri said. If he had had something scheduled, he would have canceled it. "Why don't you stop by my house for dinner at about six? After that we can talk. I want my wife Miriam to hear this too."

After Uri left, David continued toward the Western Wall. As always, the worshipers were rocking back and forth, praying for the coming of the Messiah. As David watched them, he realized that he had never had to pray that prayer one time in his entire life. He had the wonderful privilege of knowing that the Messiah had already come.

He made the ascent on up onto the Temple Mount itself. As he entered the door to the Temple Mount, his eyes fell on the Al Aqsa Mosque on the right. Al Aqsa could accommodate up to five thousand Muslim worshipers at one time. Between Al Aqsa and the Dome of the Rock was a beautiful fountain. It was here that the

Muslims washed their faces, hands, and feet before entering the mosques. On his left, he could see the beautiful Dome of the Rock. *How ironic,* David thought. *The Jews below and over in the Temple area are praying to Jehovah. The Muslims are praying to Allah. And here I am trying to convince them both about the reality of Jesus.* When he arrived at the Temple site, his first glimpse elicited a gasp from David. Though he visited the Temple Mount almost every day, he still was struck with awe at the beauty of the Third Temple.

Some Christian preachers felt that it was a horrible thing that a new Jewish Temple had been built, but David didn't feel that way. Since World War II, the world had witnessed the rebirth of the nation of Israel, the return of the Jewish people to Jerusalem, and now the building of the Third Temple. Ezekiel 37 had specifically prophesied the rebirth of Israel as a nation. The rebuilding of the Temple was also prophesied in the Scriptures. The world was actually watching a revival take place that was engineered by God Himself. One more major event had to happen to make that revival complete. But just because the revival was not yet complete did not destroy the fact that a sovereign act of God was in progress in the earth. The climactic moment would be when Jesus returned to earth to be crowned as King of kings and Lord of lords. David knew that day was not far away.

As he stepped into the outer court of the Temple, a voice beside him said, "Aren't you David Freeman?"

Turning to his left, David saw a Jewish man of about 34 years of age. He was dressed in the black suit and black hat of the Hasidic Jews. "Yes, I'm David," he replied, smiling. "And your name?"

"I'm Caleb Golden. I have been listening to many of your radio interviews. At first, you made me very angry. But after a while I became more and more interested. Now I listen every chance I get. I've learned so much from you and Roger. Thank you so much for all of your teaching."

"You're so welcome, Caleb," David replied. "If you listen to us every day, then you realize that we are Christians."

"Yes, I do realize that." Tears brimmed in Caleb's eyes as he talked. "And for some time I've been carefully considering the prophecies that indicate Jesus was the Messiah. It seemed like these things really converged in my life last night. I read Isaiah 53 through several times last evening. Every time I read it, it seemed more and more clear to me that it was speaking of Jesus. Finally, I said to God, 'If this is true, let my path cross with the path of Roger Cornell or David Freeman tomorrow.' When I saw you, I knew I had to speak to you about it."

"Caleb, that is wonderful!" David exclaimed. "God is obviously working in your life."

"What do I do now?" Caleb inquired.

"Would your schedule permit you to attend my Bible class tomorrow at one o'clock at the Mount of Olives Hotel?" David asked.

"Yes. I can be there," Caleb replied excitedly.

"Good," David said. "There will be many other new Christians there as well. I'll tell you then what you should do next."

David glanced at his watch. It was four o'clock. He had to be at Uri and Miriam's house for dinner at six. He had just enough time to stop by his hotel room so that he could freshen up and rest a few minutes.

David had taken a room at the King Solomon since it was located near the Temple Mount. As he stepped into the hotel's side entrance, his eyes swept over the lobby. For the past few weeks, he had been followed almost constantly. It had gotten to the point where he could pick the plain-clothed secret serviceman out of a crowd almost every time. At first, David didn't spot anyone. But just as he entered the elevator, he saw him. The man had positioned himself in a chair behind the big potted plant. He was reading a copy of the *Jerusalem Post*.

As the door of the elevator closed, David punched the button for the fourth floor where he was staying. Suddenly, the strongest impression came to his mind. *Don't go to your room!* He didn't hesitate. Quickly he pushed floor two. When the door opened, he walked rapidly to the end of the hall, entered the stairway, and ran down the steps, taking them two at a time. Going all the way to the basement level, he proceeded swiftly to the back employees' entrance, which exited into the garden.

David knew about this entrance because he had scouted out every possible exit from the hotel the day he had checked in. He had known that it was only a matter of time before Arachev's Global Police tried to move in on him. Moving quickly away from the hotel, he circled around to where he could observe what was going on without being seen. When he saw the ten Global Police vehicles in front of the King Solomon, he knew that the heat was on. They were undoubtedly searching through the contents of his room at this very moment.

Now what should he do? He glanced at his watch...5:15. He was supposed to be at Uri and Miriam's house by six. Was it safe to go there? Of course it would be. No one knew about the dinner arrangement except Uri and him. It was the perfect place to go until things quieted down.

David didn't dare go to his car. He knew it would be under surveillance, too. He calculated that it would take him about half an hour to walk to the address Uri had given to him.

David kept to the side streets as he made his way toward Uri's house, located in West Jerusalem. He was well aware that every single police officer in Jerusalem had been notified to be on the lookout for him. There were two major thoroughfares, Bar-Lev Avenue and Jaffa Road, that he had to cross. He would have to be careful.

Ten minutes passed without incident. David could see Bar-Lev up ahead. As usual, the road was extremely busy. "Be with me, Lord," he prayed softly. He stayed behind a tree while waiting for a break in the traffic. Finally, he was able to move swiftly across the street. *Made it*, David thought, breathing a sigh of relief. He headed down the next side street, walking in relative obscurity. That's when he saw the Global Police car. He turned up the walk to one of the residences as though he was actually going there. But it was too late.

He heard the voice of the officer from the car that had pulled over to the curb. "Sir." David had no choice but to turn. The Global Police officer said to him, "Aren't you David Freeman?"

"Yes, officer, I am." There was nothing else that David could do but tell the truth.

"Please get in the car, Mr. Freeman," the officer ordered. David got in.

As he settled into the seat, he thought, *Well, this is it. I'll be taken to the police station for questioning. Perhaps there will be beatings–maybe even some torture...*He forced himself to turn his thoughts toward Jesus. The Scripture that he had quoted to others a thousand times now came to his mind. "And we know that all things work together for good to them that love God, to them who are the called according to His purpose." With that, David's calm assurance returned. *No matter what happens, everything will be all right. God is in total control, no matter how dark things look*, he thought.

The officer turned to David. "Mr. Freeman, do you know that there has been a worldwide warrant issued for your arrest?"

"No, officer. I didn't know that," David replied. "Can you tell me the basis for this warrant?"

The officer looked at the computer screen mounted in the dash of his car. "It says here that you are charged with crimes against humanity, and specifically with widespread religious proselytizing. As you know, that was made a very serious offense under the new hate crime laws."

"Officer, do you agree with these new laws that infringe so drastically on our personal liberties?" David inquired.

The officer's expression softened. "Actually, David, I am not arresting you. You see, I was baptized by your partner, Roger Cornell, about four months ago. However, you should know that you are in danger. Now, where do you need to go? I will take you."

Officer Friedman dropped David off two blocks from Uri and Miriam's house so he could truthfully say that he didn't know where David had gone—if he were ever questioned.

The dinner that Miriam had prepared was delicious. David didn't want to frighten Uri and Miriam, but he wondered to himself if he might be eating jail food by this time tomorrow.

Uri and Miriam could hardly eat their dinner for asking questions. It was obvious that Uri had been talking to Miriam about the things he and David had discussed earlier in the day.

Miriam turned to David. "I see the prophecies that appear to have been fulfilled by the coming of Jesus. But there's one thing I still don't understand. What about all the prophecies that talk about the Messiah establishing His kingdom on earth? What about peace on earth and the lion lying down with the lamb?"

"You know, Miriam, those are the very questions that caused many people to reject Jesus as the Messiah. Some still say, 'If Jesus was the Messiah, why haven't we had peace on earth?' That is confusing to people because they do not understand that the Messiah was to come to earth twice. He came the first time as the Lamb of God to take away the sin of the world. He will soon come again as the Lion of the tribe of Judah. It's at His Second Coming that the rest of the prophecies will be fulfilled. The reason so many people missed the First Coming is because they did not distinguish between the sufferings of Messiah and the glories that will come at the time of His Second Coming."

David, Uri, and Miriam talked late into the night. As a matter of fact, David became so engrossed in teaching about Jesus that he totally forgot his own predicament. When he glanced at his watch, it was 12:00 midnight.

David quickly rose to his feet. "Uri, Miriam—I'd better get going. I didn't realize it was this late. Forgive me for staying so long."

Miriam quickly replied, "Don't feel bad at all. We've enjoyed every minute of it. When can we get together again? We definitely need to learn a lot more." They agreed together that they would touch base the next day.

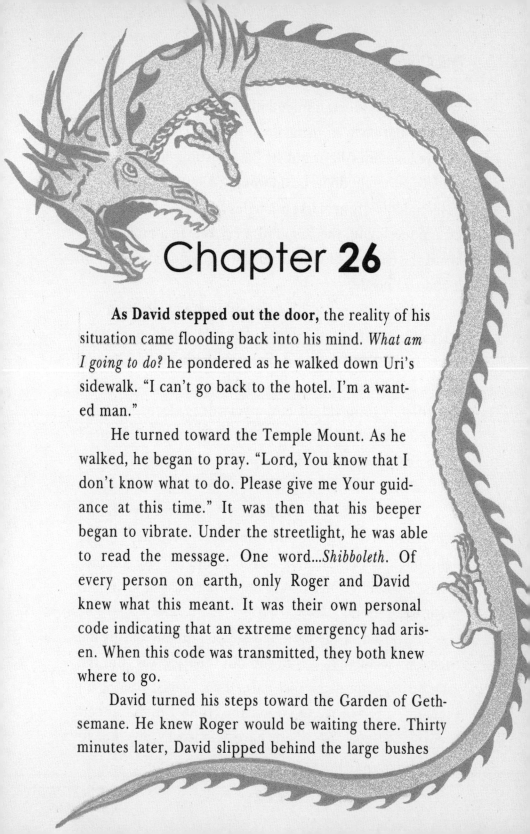

Chapter 26

As David stepped out the door, the reality of his situation came flooding back into his mind. *What am I going to do?* he pondered as he walked down Uri's sidewalk. "I can't go back to the hotel. I'm a wanted man."

He turned toward the Temple Mount. As he walked, he began to pray. "Lord, You know that I don't know what to do. Please give me Your guidance at this time." It was then that his beeper began to vibrate. Under the streetlight, he was able to read the message. One word...*Shibboleth*. Of every person on earth, only Roger and David knew what this meant. It was their own personal code indicating that an extreme emergency had arisen. When this code was transmitted, they both knew where to go.

David turned his steps toward the Garden of Gethsemane. He knew Roger would be waiting there. Thirty minutes later, David slipped behind the large bushes growing along the wall surrounding the part of the garden that was not open to the general public. There he waited. In a few minutes he heard it: the whistling like a bird as only Roger could do it. David would recognize that whistle in the middle of the darkest jungles of Africa. David made his unique sound, the sound of a cricket. In a moment he heard the clicking of the garden gate. He moved quickly to it and slid inside.

Roger appeared at his side and immediately began to relay the events of the night. He told David about his interrupted plans to spend the night with Eli and Naomi Levi. "I went to bed at my normal time of 11 o'clock. I immediately dropped off into a very deep sleep. At exactly 12 midnight I was suddenly wide awake. I never do that! Once I'm asleep, I'm asleep for the entire night." David nodded.

"When I woke up, I immediately had the overriding impression that I should leave the house. I reached for the light, but a voice said, 'No!' David, I can't tell you whether it was an audible voice or whether it was just in my mind, but it was very real.

"I dressed in the dark and slipped quietly out of the room. My inclination was to slip out the back way. But the same strong impression that warned me against turning on the light, directed me to go out the front. I didn't understand it, but you and I both have learned by now not to ever disobey that voice."

"And you know, Roger, the more dangerous things get for us, the more important it will be for us to never disregard that voice," David added.

Roger continued with his story. "As I walked down the front walk, I spotted the plain car that I knew belonged to the secret police."

"Are you serious?!" David interrupted. "What did you do?"

"Believe it or not, I walked right by it as though nothing was wrong."

"And what happened?" David asked incredulously.

"I couldn't believe it! The guy in the car was dead asleep! I waited till I was a safe distance away. Then I put the call through to your beeper."

"Roger, that secret service man could be given the death penalty by Arachev for dereliction of duty!" David remarked. "Apparently God just put him into a deep sleep! Isn't it amazing how He has looked out for us?"

David then told Roger about the secret service man in the lobby of the King Solomon. When he told his partner about circling around to see all the global police cars in front, Roger said, "Then they have decided to arrest both of us."

"It certainly looks that way," David replied. "We need God's guidance on what we should do now."

"Well, what are our options?" Roger mused. "We could flee the country, but they would probably catch us at the border. We could try to go underground, but then our work would come to a halt. We're just going to have to pray until we know exactly what God wants us to do."

Roger and David spent the rest of the night praying there in the Garden of Gethsemane. More than once during the night, Roger was sure that he sensed the presence of Jesus Himself with them. He had never had a prayer meeting quite like that one. It was a wonderful experience to pray the night through in the same place where Jesus had prayed before His crucifixion.

As the sun started to peek over the Mount of Olives, Roger and David concluded their prayers. "What do you think God would have us to do?" David asked Roger.

"Do you remember in the Bible what God told the disciples to do after they had been miraculously delivered from jail?" Roger asked.

"You mean when they were instructed to go stand in the Temple and speak the words of life to the people?" David responded.

"Exactly," Roger said. "I believe God wants us to go boldly to our normal preaching point on the Mount of Olives and preach to the people. That's what I feel like God wants us to do."

"You've got to be kidding!" David protested. "We would be sitting ducks if we did that."

"You're the one who said that we must always listen to God's voice, no matter what," Roger reminded. "If you don't feel that's what God wants you to do, then don't do it. But I'm sure that's what God wants me to do."

David smiled weakly. "To tell you the truth, that's exactly what I felt God speaking to my heart all night, but I kept pushing it away. I think we'd better just obey what God has spoken to both of us." He paused. "You know, Roger, this whole thing is about over. Have you taken a look at your calendar lately?"

"What do you mean?" Roger asked.

David explained, "Do you realize how long it's been since Arachev stood in the Temple claiming to be the Messiah?"

Roger quickly calculated in his mind. "Unbelievable! It's been just about three-and-a-half years! We've been so busy preaching, teaching, and writing that I had lost track. No wonder Arachev is closing in on us! It's time for this whole thing to wrap up."

Roger and David slipped down the side of the house of one of the little-known, but well-trusted disciples. When Lydia opened the back door, she was surprised to see the two men of God. "Come in," she said immediately. "Where have you two been? All the believers have been so worried about you. Do you know that several hundred of our people were arrested in Arachev's sting operation last night? We thought perhaps they had gotten the two of you as well."

"They would have if God had not intervened. They attempted to arrest both of us," David explained.

"Both of you certainly look like you've had a rough night," Lydia observed. "Why don't you grab a shower while I fix some breakfast? By the time you get cleaned up, it will be ready."

As they sat down to the table a short time later, David mentioned to Lydia what had dawned on them in the garden. "We just realized it has been almost three-and-a-half years since Arachev made his messianic claim. You know the Bible says that's how long the antichrist will be permitted to continue."

Lydia's eyes grew wide with excitement. "I probably should tell you what was on the news this morning. The United Nations has decided to send the forces of the World Community into Israel to settle the dispute over Jerusalem once and for all. Does that mean anything?"

"Does it mean anything?!" David exclaimed. "I'll tell you what it means! It means we are on the brink of the Battle of Armageddon! I know what we're going to be preaching about today. We must get a message to our Internet contacts immediately. It looks like today is the day that we deliver the final warning!"

Roger and David made their way to the Mount of Olives. Apparently Arachev and the Global Police never dreamed that they would show up at their regular preaching point since warrants had been issued for their arrests. With the news that morning filled with stories about the arrests of the Endtimers, no one expected to see Roger and David out in public—and on the Mount of Olives, of all places! When the crowd saw the two preachers, they immediately began to gather around.

Roger opened his Bible to Revelation 16:15-16 and read, "Behold, I come as a thief. Blessed is he that watcheth, and keepeth his garments, lest he walk naked, and they see his shame. And he gathered them together into a place called in the Hebrew tongue Armageddon."

Roger looked around at the crowd with a boldness he had never felt before. "The title of my sermon today will be 'Final Warning.'" A murmur swept through the crowd. Eyebrows were lifted as the impact of the sermon title drove itself home in each person's mind.

Sensing that he had the crowd's undivided attention, Roger began to speak. "David Freeman and I have been preaching for the last three-and-one-half years about events that have occurred here on earth and about those things soon to come. The things we have been warning you about are now upon us."

"Slightly over three-and-a-half years ago, we told you that a time of great religious persecution would begin when a global political leader stood in the Third Temple claiming to be the Messiah. A few days after that warning, Michael Arachev stood in the Temple and claimed to be Messiah and God. All of you have since witnessed the religious and political oppression that we warned you about.

"At that same time, we told you that this time of persecution, called the Great Tribulation in the Bible, would last for three and one-half years. Check your calendars. That time is now complete.

"During the time of our preaching, we have taught repeatedly that all of these events would culminate with the Battle of Gog and Magog, also known as the Battle of Armageddon. We have been very specific that the Battle of Armageddon would be triggered by the invasion of Israel by the forces of the World Community. If you listened to your news this morning, the forces of the World Community are, at this moment, gathered on the banks of the Euphrates River preparing to invade Israel.

"Ladies and gentlemen, we stand today on the brink of the Battle of Armageddon and the Second Coming of Jesus to this earth. The time has arrived for the fulfillment of the Scripture that I read a few moments ago. Let's read it again: 'Behold, I come as a thief. Blessed is he that watcheth, and keepeth his garments, lest he walk naked, and they see his shame. And he gathered them together into a place called in the Hebrew tongue Armageddon.'

"My dear brothers and sisters, this is your final warning. If you have not yet been born again, you must do it before this day is over! Please do not disregard this message. This is your final warning!"

In the urgency of the moment, David and Roger did not notice the Global Police converging on them from their left. As soon as the crowd saw the police, they scattered in every direction. David heard the lead officer shout, "There they are. Get them!"

Out of the corner of his eye, Roger saw Attorney General Suslov. Suslov had been livid when he realized that both Cornell and Freeman had eluded him. It had been so humiliating since he had promised Arachev that they would be arrested. Suslov did not like being humiliated!

Roger was shocked when he saw Suslov pull the machine pistol from beneath his trench coat. As the bullets ripped through his body, Roger's eyes looked upward from the Mount of Olives toward the sky. His last thought was, *Resurrection—three-and-a-half days.*

When Suslov had told Arachev the day before that both Cornell and Freeman had eluded them, he actually thought Arachev would have a heart attack. Suslov had never seen him so angry. It was only then that Suslov realized how much raw hatred was bottled up inside this man toward the two preachers who had brought such havoc to the New World Order. It was therefore with great satisfaction that Suslov pulled his cell phone from his pocket and placed the call to Arachev's private number. When Arachev answered, Suslov merely said, "Mr. President, Cornell and Freeman are dead."

For a moment there was silence on the other end...then jubilation. "Terrific, Suslov!" Arachev almost shouted. "I knew I could count on you. Great job!"

"Mr. President, what should we do with the bodies?" Suslov asked.

"Where are they now?" Arachev inquired.

"Lying here in the street on the top of the Mount of Olives. You know—where they always came to preach," Suslov informed him.

"Are you telling me that Cornell and Freeman were up there preaching in broad daylight, knowing that we had issued warrants for their arrests?" Arachev questioned incredulously. "How stupid could they be?"

"Listen, Suslov," Arachev continued, "since Cornell and Freeman liked to go up there to preach so much, I think we should leave them lying right there for all to see. Place the bodies under guard day and night. Let the whole world see that they are dead. We won't leave any room for any more of their hocus pocus. We'll hold the spot open to public view for four days so that no one can conjure up fantastic stories about their rising from the dead after three-and-a-half days. That's the rumor going around."

Hmm. Suslov thought. *Arachev hated these guys' guts!* "Will do, sir," he said aloud, and flipped the cell phone shut.

Turning to Solano, Suslov ordered, "Pick your most trusted men to guard these bodies. They are to remain on public display for the next four days. Have no less than six men on guard around the clock. If anything happens to these two bodies, it will mean the death penalty for those on duty."

In less than 30 minutes, CNN, BBC, Reuters, and most of the other news services were swarming the Mount of Olives. The pictures of the bullet-riddled bodies of Roger Cornell and David Freeman were instantly broadcast around the world.

Chapter **27**

*And the sixth angel poured out his vial upon the
great river Euphrates; and the water thereof was
dried up, that the way of the kings of the east
might be prepared....And he gathered them
together into a place called in the Hebrew
tongue Armageddon.* Revelation 16:12,16

Inside the control room of Turkey's Ataturk
Dam, Omer Tariq waited tensely for the call to
come. He checked his watch—8:30 p.m. It should be
anytime now. Though he was expecting it, the fateful ringing of the phone still caused him to leap
with a start from his chair. The voice on the other
end gave the required passwords—"three wise men."
Omer hung up the phone and immediately began
the routine that would raise the dam, totally cutting off
the flow of the Euphrates. In 15 minutes, the huge,
surging river had slowed to a trickle.

By 11 p.m., the water in the Euphrates at the chosen crossing point had dried up. The weather forecast was right on the money—overcast skies, no moonlight, with heavy fog. Air reconnaissance and spy satellites were worthless.

The tanks, half-tracks, bulldozers, and troop transports began to move quickly across the river bed. The commander of the International Forces, Vladimir Zhuganov, watched proudly as the operation proceeded virtually without a hitch. By midnight, the dash for the northern border of Israel had begun.

At top speed, the trip from the Euphrates to Damascus, Syria, would take about four hours. As the convoy moved southward and westward, some of the troops tried to catch a few winks of sleep. Others talked.

Nikoli Anderov, a young soldier from the Ukraine, turned to Boris Ustinov from Russia. "You think this operation will be over in a few days like they are telling us?"

Ustinov shrugged. "Sure. Why not? No one can stand before the might of the World Community. Milosevic learned that the hard way! You agree?"

Nikoli shrugged tentatively. "I don't know. You would think so. But I got a call from my mother two days ago when she learned I was being sent to fight in Israel. She begged me to do everything I could to get out of being part of this operation. She claimed that this was going to be the Battle of Armageddon prophesied in the Bible."

"Was she serious?" Boris asked incredulously.

"Yeah, man. She even tried to talk me into going AWOL!" Nikoli half laughed. "I told her that would get me court martialed, but still she didn't care. I've never seen her act so crazy about anything before."

"I don't believe in all that Bible prophecy junk. I wouldn't worry about it, if I were you. You know how superstitious old people are about their religion." Boris tried to act cocksure of himself, but Nikoli thought he heard a little fear in Boris's voice.

"Boris, have you ever heard anything about this supposed Battle of Armageddon?" Nikoli questioned.

"Oh, I've heard of it before, all right. But I don't believe it for a minute," Boris replied. "Hey, man, this conversation's starting to get on my nerves. We'd better grab some sleep."

Boris turned onto his left side, stuffing his jacket under his head for a pillow. But Nikoli was wide awake now. His mind was racing like a runaway freight train. "Armageddon...blood to the horses' bridles...winepress of the wrath of God...a heavenly army on white horses..." What he had learned at church as a young boy all came flooding back. Was he getting ready to fight against Jesus Christ Himself? Nikoli noticed that Boris wasn't sleeping much either. First he turned this way and then that. Nikoli actually thought about trying to pray as the convoy raced toward its appointment in the Plain of Megiddo.

Around 4 a.m. the first of the International Forces began to wind its way through Damascus. The Golan

Heights were reached by 5 a.m. "Right on schedule," Zhuganov proudly observed.

The trip across the Golan Heights was a piece of cake. The Syrian Defense Minister, Maher Hassad, grinned at Zhuganov. "If it weren't for the agreement that returned the Golan to Syria, we'd be fighting for our lives right now. People say that the Jews are so smart, winning all those Nobel and Pulitzer prizes and all. Do you know what we gave them for all this priceless territory? A piece of paper! One pathetic piece of paper with President Zahmud's signature on it! And Zahmud made them think he was doing them a favor! For one piece of paper, Israel gave us this entire territory so critical to her security. Without the Golan, this invasion would be absolutely impossible. But Zahmud wore them down. He just waited and waited while the international community kept putting the pressure on."

By daybreak the most powerful army to ever invade the nation of Israel stood poised to unleash all its fury on the northern border. The plan was to strike at first light and move as fast as possible to the Plain of Megiddo. Naval forces would simultaneously launch an invasion from the Mediterranean Sea near the Port of Haifa. The two forces would meet at Megiddo. Zhuganov turned to Hassad. "I've heard that Megiddo is the place from which Armageddon gets its name. Is that true?"

"Yes. You know that Lord Allenby, who invaded Israel during World War I, was given the title Lord of

Armageddon. At the time he actually thought he was fighting the Battle of Armageddon."

"Really?" Zhuganov replied. "Well, we don't have to worry about anything like the mythical Battle of Armageddon. The Israelis don't stand a chance. We have them so outmanned and outgunned that they won't know what hit them."

Hassad's mood suddenly turned dark and serious. "It's obvious you've never fought the Israelis before. I have. Strange things happen when you fight against them. It may not be as easy as you anticipate."

His first view of the beautiful Sea of Galilee almost took Zhuganov's breath away when he topped the last hill of the Golan. *If this is what the Promised Land looks like, no wonder men have been fighting over it for four thousand years!* Eight miles long and thirteen miles wide, the Sea of Galilee lay like a haven of peace in the middle of a turbulent, violent world. *So this was where Jesus walked on the water...or so they say.* The City of Tiberius nestled beautifully on the southwest end of the Galilee. Looking at the City of Tiberius, named after Tiberius Caesar, created a certain sense of awe in the commander's heart. *What a historical place! Caesar and Jesus, Capernaum and Bethesda...* Zhuganov jerked his thoughts back to the task at hand. "We're going to make a little history of our own today," he told himself. "We're going to remove the last obstacle to our longtime dream of the New World Order!"

The element of surprise that the forces of the international community achieved by the drying up of the Euphrates was almost complete. That maneuver was an absolute stroke of genius. Israel was simply unprepared for the massive attack that now plunged across her border, totally eradicating all resistance in its way. The Israeli Army had no choice but to fall back to the Plain of Megiddo to set up its defense.

When Zhuganov's command vehicle topped the hill overlooking Megiddo, he could literally feel the rush of adrenaline that surged through his body. What an absolutely perfect theater for war! Seven kilometers wide, fifteen kilometers long, and mountains on every side. No wonder some of the world's most famous battles had been fought there.

Already a ferocious tank battle was in progress out in the valley. The roar was deafening. Jets screamed overhead as they attempted to support their tank units. Now this was war!

As the international force from Haifa entered Megiddo from the western side, the Israelis suddenly realized they were fighting a two-front war. Knowing how deadly that can be, the Israeli armored unit began to drive southeast toward the mouth of the Jordan Valley. Having anticipated this move, the Russian troops were there to head them off. However, an Israeli unit coming up the Jordan Valley from the south allowed Israel to break through, creating an escape route for its forces trapped at Megiddo.

Zhuganov had to admire the Israeli troops. Repeatedly, he was sure that certain Israeli units were trapped with no way out when suddenly some kind of brilliant maneuver would allow the unit to reconnect with Israel's main forces. So this was the vaunted Israeli individual initiative he had heard so much about! Not that it mattered. He would grind them down, kilometer after torturous kilometer.

Israeli soldiers knew every inch of their terrain, and they knew how to exploit it to the maximum. Yet, little by little, the Israeli Army had to retreat down the Jordan Valley—closer and closer to Jerusalem.

In her long and turbulent history, Israel had never seen an invasion that compared to this onslaught of the World Community. The level of firepower brought to bear upon the tiny nation of Israel was so overwhelming that it pushed soldiers to the brink of insanity. And the attacks were so unrelenting! The Russian troops, who played the dominant role in this invasion force, had that same tenacity that had brought the mighty Nazi juggernaut to a grinding halt.

The speed of the advance of the global forces was stunning. The Israeli Army, as always, fought brilliantly. The closer to Jerusalem the enemy came, the more desperate the resistance became. Just when it would seem that the conflict had reached its highest possible intensity, somehow it would be ratcheted up even higher.

When the global forces advanced to within 20 kilometers of Jerusalem, the highest of Israel's military officials and political leaders gathered at command headquarters to determine the final strategy for Israel's last stand.

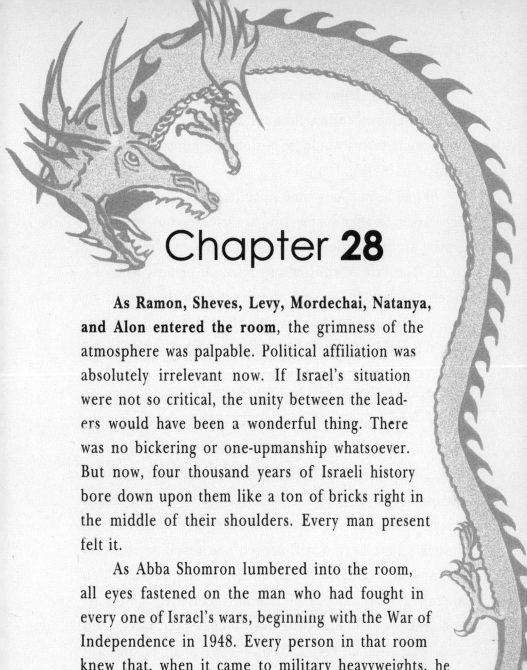

Chapter 28

As Ramon, Sheves, Levy, Mordechai, Natanya, and Alon entered the room, the grimness of the atmosphere was palpable. Political affiliation was absolutely irrelevant now. If Israel's situation were not so critical, the unity between the leaders would have been a wonderful thing. There was no bickering or one-upmanship whatsoever. But now, four thousand years of Israeli history bore down upon them like a ton of bricks right in the middle of their shoulders. Every man present felt it.

As Abba Shomron lumbered into the room, all eyes fastened on the man who had fought in every one of Israel's wars, beginning with the War of Independence in 1948. Every person in that room knew that, when it came to military heavyweights, he was the warrior giant of the modern nation of Israel. What was he thinking? Was there one more brilliant plan behind those shrewd eyes?

Israel was almost out of options, and they all knew it. Israeli intelligence was telling them that, by the end of this day, enemy forces would be within five kilometers of the walls of Jerusalem.

It had been a long time since Israel's Chief Rabbi had been asked to attend a meeting at this level; but, given the gravity of the situation, it had seemed to be the right thing to do. The Prime Minister surprised all present when he asked the Rabbi to open the meeting with a word of prayer. However, not one voice of dissent was raised to this suggestion. Even to the most secular Zionist in the room, the prayer was appreciated.

Rabbi Richman's voice was deep with emotion as he began. "O Lord our God, God of Abraham, Isaac, and Jacob, we have sinned. We have disregarded Your instruction, and we have every man done that which was right in his own eyes. As a result, we have come to our present calamity. Now, O Lord, we come begging Your forgiveness. We have been a stiff-necked and rebellious people. But now we remember Your words, 'If My people, which are called by My name, shall humble themselves, and pray, and seek My face, and turn from their wicked ways; then will I hear from heaven, and will forgive their sin, and will heal their land.' O Lord God, hear us! Forgive us! Heal our backslidings. At this time, grant wisdom and insight to these our leaders that they may lead Your people Israel through this valley of our darkest hour. Amen."

As the bowed heads raised, you could almost see the change taking place in the hearts of the men in the room. The Prime Minister stood. "Thank you, Rabbi. Every word you prayed was true. Your prayer may have been the most important thing on our agenda today."

When it was time for discussions to begin, you could see the wheels turning in the great minds sitting around the conference table. Eyes moved from one man to the other. Thoughts raced. *How did we get to where we are?*

There was Simon Sheves, the elder statesman. Every person in the room knew that he truly loved Israel. He had given his life to the service of the country. Yet now it was obvious that his dovish views had been terribly misguided. Even as this meeting began, Israeli soldiers were paying a terrible price for every inch of ground that Sheves' policies had advocated giving away.

Across from Sheves sat Yoni Natanya. It was Yoni who had cut the legs out from under the Likud, the party that stood against territorial compromise. Not only did Natanya fulfill the Oslo Accords, but he also negotiated the Wye Agreement, which ultimately brought the horrible slaughter down upon the heads of the Judean settlers.

Then there was Ramon, the man who had inadvertently shocked the nation of Israel back to her senses. Ramon had offered to re-divide Jerusalem and even surrender sovereignty over the Temple Mount. The people of Israel couldn't believe that any Israeli Prime Minister would offer to surrender forever their holiest place, the

Temple Mount. Even harder to believe was that Palestinian leader Yasser Arafat had turned down Ramon's offer. That's when the Israelis knew that nothing short of the destruction of their nation would satisfy the Palestinians.

Finally, Shomron the bulldozer. He was the man whom Israel turned to when nothing else worked. It was Shomron who assumed the southern command when Israel teetered on the brink of defeat in the Yom Kippur War of 1973. He had been brought out of forced retirement when the magnitude of Israel's disaster became apparent. His bold maneuver across the Suez Canal, encircling Egypt's army, put Israel back on the offensive where she fought best. As a result, Israel's enemies were soon petitioning the UN to broker a cease-fire. Having fought in every war since 1948, he knew what Israel was facing better than any man in the room.

As the discussions began, Shomron sat quietly in his chair—listening, thinking, observing. Plan after plan was offered by those sitting around the table. Sheves suggested, "Get the United States to demand a cease-fire at the UN."

Natanya, who had served as Israel's UN ambassador, shook his head slowly. "It won't work. It's the UN we are fighting. They're winning, so they have no reason to want a cease-fire."

Forever the strategist, Ramon suggested, "Can we cross into Jordan in order to encircle the Global Forces, cutting their lines of supply?"

Eyes swung to the Defense Minister. "Can it be done?"

"It's impossible. We are fighting for our very lives. We don't have one unit to spare. Gentlemen, the situation is that our nation will make its last stand tomorrow." The Defense Minister's words drove home like a sixteen-pound sledgehammer. Israel's back was against the wall.

You could almost see the thoughts racing through each mind. *What if we lose? Are we on the brink of another Masada? Worst yet, could Israel be headed for another holocaust?* Israelis had hoped those days were over forever. However, recent actions by the World Community had jarred every Israeli back to reality. Yes, this world was still capable of marching Jews to gas chambers. The ruthless slaughter that Israel had suffered over the last few days provided indisputable proof of that fact to every person in the room.

There were only black clouds on the horizon. It seemed there was no help anywhere. As eyes slid searchingly from man to man, it suddenly dawned on everyone present that Abba Shomron had not said a word.

The night before Shomron had sat staring into his fireplace till the wee hours of the morning. He had turned every possible battlefield scenario over and over in his mind. One by one, he rejected them. He believed that Israel had the finest armed forces on the face of the earth, but attempting to take on the entire world was asking them to do the impossible. By 4 o'clock in the morning, Shomron had been able to come up with only one answer.

The Prime Minister turned to Shomron. "Abba, what do you think? What can we do?"

The reply came without hesitation. "The Samson Option."

The impact of Shomron's words hit every man right in the gut! A deadly silence filled the room. Finally, Sheves broke the silence. "Abba, you think our only option is to go nuclear? You're talking about the point of no return!"

Shomron's reply was immediate. "We are already at the point of no return, Simon. Do you remember what you were thinking when you convinced the French to sell us the Dimona nuclear reactor? None of us wanted to be a nuclear power! But all of us had learned through four thousand years of Jewish history that this day would probably come. That's why you played every card in your hand to obtain nuclear weapons for Israel. You may yet prove to be the savior of our nation, Simon."

Israel had never officially acknowledged to the world that she possessed nuclear weapons. However, she had said that, if Israel did have nuclear capability, those weapons would be used only if the nation's existence was in danger.

When Israel's legendary judge Samson died, he took the house of the Philistine lords down with him. Thus, it had just seemed appropriate that Israel's nuclear capability should bear the same name—"The Samson Option."

Every man in that room had hoped this day would never come. But all of them knew that Abba Shomron had forced them to face the truth. The only choice they had was "The Samson Option."

Chapter 29

Arachev had been certain that eliminating the two leaders of the Bible believers' movement would take the steam right out of the surging religious awakening. Instead, it did the exact opposite.

The morning after Cornell and Freeman had been killed, the Internet Police brought the intercepted messages that were being sent around the world by the Endtimers. Arachev did not fully grasp the implications of what he was reading.

The messages went like this:

"The two prophets whom God sent to the earth for the endtime are dead. All of you know the prophecy about these two witnesses, found in Revelation 11:9-12: 'And they of the people and kindreds and tongues and nations shall see their dead bodies three days and an half, and shall not suffer their dead bodies to be put in graves....And after three days and an half the Spirit of life from God entered into them, and they stood upon their feet; and great fear fell upon them which saw them. And they heard a great voice from heaven saying unto them, Come up hither. And they ascended up to heaven in a cloud; and their enemies beheld them.'

"True to this prophecy, Arachev has ordered that the bodies of Roger Cornell and David Freeman are to be left to rot in the streets. What Arachev doesn't know is that they will, in fact, rise from the dead in three-and-a-half days. That's also when the seventh and last trumpet sounds. It appears that we are three days away from the Second Coming. Whatever we are going to do for the cause of Jesus must be done in the next three days!"

The surging revival turned into a tidal wave! The Bible believers worked around the clock without sleep. There were more conversions in the next three days than had occurred in any year since the beginning of the Christian Church. It was estimated that ten million people were born again while their leaders lay dead on the Mount of Olives.

In the meantime, WNN carried its noon report concerning Cornell and Freeman each day. The cameras zoomed in on the dead bodies of the two preachers while government-hired demonstrators celebrated in the background. Around the world, those who had taken the mark of the beast were filled with elation. They would gather before the television at noon, and, when the images of Cornell and Freeman's bodies came on the screen, they would cheer and rejoice because of this great victory for the New World Order. The hatred that these followers of Arachev had toward the two preachers was unearthly. As a matter of fact, it was demonic.

After Cornell and Freeman had been dead for two days, Suslov and Arachev sat together at world headquarters viewing the noon report of the two bodies on the Mount of Olives. "So much for their soon-coming kingdom of God now," Arachev gloated as he watched the orchestrated celebrations taking place around the bodies of Cornell and Freeman. "Once the prophesied three days and a half pass with no resurrection, we'll be done with these right-wing prophecy demagogues. Once that prophecy doesn't come to pass, their followers will dissipate and fade into oblivion. Suslov, 'ol buddy, thanks to you I won't have to worry about this end-time element anymore."

Even while basking beneath Arachev's rarely given praise, one thing haunted Suslov. The bodies of Cornell and Freeman were not swelling.

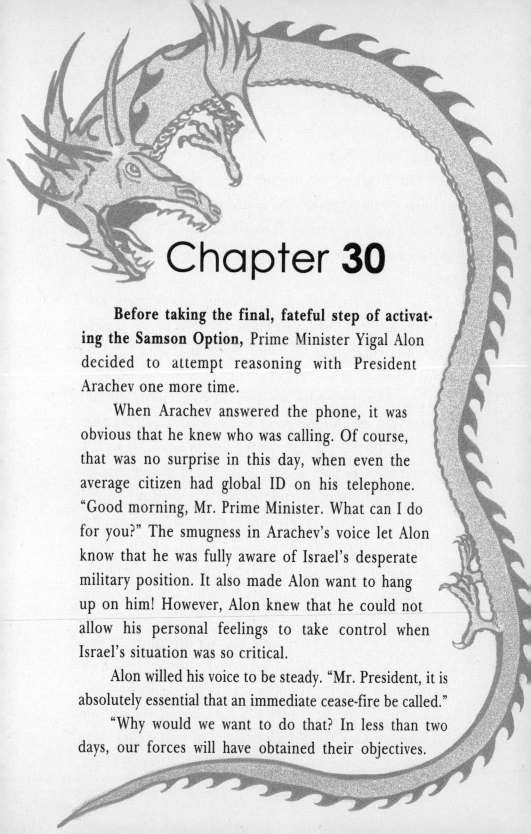

Chapter **30**

Before taking the final, fateful step of activating the Samson Option, Prime Minister Yigal Alon decided to attempt reasoning with President Arachev one more time.

When Arachev answered the phone, it was obvious that he knew who was calling. Of course, that was no surprise in this day, when even the average citizen had global ID on his telephone. "Good morning, Mr. Prime Minister. What can I do for you?" The smugness in Arachev's voice let Alon know that he was fully aware of Israel's desperate military position. It also made Alon want to hang up on him! However, Alon knew that he could not allow his personal feelings to take control when Israel's situation was so critical.

Alon willed his voice to be steady. "Mr. President, it is absolutely essential that an immediate cease-fire be called."

"Why would we want to do that? In less than two days, our forces will have obtained their objectives.

Why would we want to stop now?" Arachev's voice sounded as though it were made of steel—cold, hard steel.

The Israeli Prime Minister's voice trembled as he spoke. "Mr. Arachev, you are forcing me to make decisions that I don't want to make. These decisions will have dreadful consequences for your forces and ours. We need to stop this conflict before everything spins totally out of control!"

"Mr. Prime Minister, perhaps things are spinning out of control for you, but I assure you that everything is perfectly under control on our side," Arachev replied, sounding as cool as a cucumber. Then his voice became menacing. "I strongly advise you not to do anything stupid. We know your capabilities down to the dotting of the i and the crossing of the t. Your only course of action is to lay down your arms and bring your nation into full compliance with the resolutions of the international community."

Alon took a deep breath and decided to try one more line of reasoning, "Mr. President, we in Israel always thought that you were our friend. Now it looks like you are determined to destroy our nation. Why are you doing this?"

Arachev's answer came back without hesitation. It was obvious he had rehearsed his logic many times. "I tried to be a friend to Israel, but you would never blend into the World Community. You always had to be different. You think you are God's chosen people, and that belief contaminates everything that you do. Whether you Jews admit it or not, you really think you are better than everyone else. When almost every nation on earth signed the Nuclear Non-proliferation Treaty, you refused to sign it. When the United Nations voted 150-2 that Jerusalem was not Israel's capital but an international city under UN protection, you refused to accept it. You think your religion is right and everyone else's is wrong.

"This is a dangerous world we live in. We almost allowed it to be destroyed in the China conflict. The common good must now take precedence over everything. I am not going to allow any nation to defy the will of our world democracy—the United Nations."

Alon's reply was very measured. "Sir, you are asking us to do things that we just can't do."

"Mr. Prime Minister, you *can* do them. You are just not willing to do them," Arachev shot back emphatically. "And since Israel is not willing to do what is necessary, we will take over your country and do it for you!"

When Alon hung up, it felt like there was lead in the pit of his stomach. Yet at the same time, he strangely felt a new resolution in his heart.

Israel's Security Cabinet was to reconvene in about 15 minutes. When they entered the room, every person knew by the expression on Alon's face the outcome of the Prime Minister's conversation with the Global Leader.

Alon's words were scarce and to the point. "Gentlemen, each of you know your role in implementing the Samson Option. Move quickly. It will be launched at the appropriate time tomorrow." His words fell like a ton of bricks, even though every person there had expected to hear them.

Chairs scraped on the floor as each man rose to leave. The Prime Minister's voice rang out, "One more moment, please. There's something I have never done since becoming your leader three years ago, but I feel I should do it now. The reason Israel even exists is because of our God. Without Him, we really cannot justify the founding of the modern state of Israel. As your leader, I would like to lead you in prayer."

The room fell silent, and Alon began, "Lord God, many of us in this room have witnessed the rebirth of the nation of Israel after almost two thousand years of exile. We all know that event was nothing short of a miracle. We have seen You do many other miraculous things in the short life of this young nation. It is obvious that we need You now, possibly, as we have never needed You before. We realize that we are at a juncture very much like the one when our forefathers crossed the Red Sea. They had to have divine intervention then, and we have to have it now. Lord, we as Israel's leaders will do our best. But at the same time, we acknowledge that unless You help us, all our efforts will be in vain. We now ask for Your mercy and protection on the people of Israel." The Prime Minister hesitated, and then concluded. "And one more thing, Lord God. We know that it is promised that our Messiah will come to save us. We humbly ask that He would come to us at this time, for You know better than we do how badly we need Him. Amen."

Alon was surprised when he heard every voice around the table join in with his own "Amen." He thought, *This crisis is not only changing me; I think it's changing our entire nation.*

At 8 p.m. that evening, Prime Minister Alon spoke to the people of Israel. "My fellow countrymen, greetings. I spoke with President Arachev today, requesting a cease-fire in order to give diplomacy time to work. Mr. Arachev did not give a favorable response to my request. In fact, he expressed confidence that the military might of the World Community would force Israel's surrender within the next two days.

"The Israeli Defense Forces have fought valiantly, as always. However, it has been an unprecedented challenge for us to face the might of the entire world. No Israeli army has ever been called upon to face such a daunting task. In spite of these formidable obstacles, we will not give up. The faith and the courage that brought our ancestors out of Egypt, out of Babylon, and out of Nazi Germany, yet live on in our hearts. We will not give up.

"Not only are the people of Israel a great people, but more importantly, the God of Israel is a mighty God. He is the only true God. He brought us out of Egypt, through the Red Sea, across the Jordan River, and in modern times has restored us to this land.

"We will not surrender to this Babylonian system of one-world government that has invaded our nation. In the words of King David, 'Some trust in chariots, and some in horses: but we will remember the name of the Lord our God.'

"My fellow citizens, I ask you this evening before you retire to pray unto the Lord God of Israel that He will intervene in our behalf at this hour. May the God of Abraham, Isaac, and Jacob be with you. Good night."

In every home in Israel that evening, prayer was made. Mothers gathered children around the bedside to pray for Daddy who was out facing the enemy with the Israeli army. Elderly men slipped down on their knees before sliding into bed. Most eyes were moistened with tears by the time they turned out the lights.

God saw what was happening throughout Israel that night, and He heard their prayers. He looked down on the actions of President Arachev and the World Community, and His fury came up in His face.

Chapter **31**

The grinding, relentless attack of the Global Forces started the assault on Jerusalem at the break of dawn. The Israeli fighters was more determined than ever to resist. Still, they found themselves slowly being driven back, step by torturous step. By noon, the forces of the World Community were two kilometers from the outskirts of Jerusalem.

Prime Minister Alon was in constant contact with Israeli Defense Minister Yael Arens. Alon knew that the moment of the fateful decision couldn't be put off much longer. "Yael, what's the situation?"

"Mr. Prime Minister, our men are fighting heroically. But it's not enough. The odds are just too overwhelming! We could use a deliverer like Samson right now."

Alon's voice was as steady as an oak tree. "I'll see if I can't convince Samson to give you a hand."

All the preparations had been made in advance. The soldier commissioned to signal the launching of the Samson Option was by the Prime Minister's side. As soon as Alon hung up the phone, he gave one nod in the officer's direction. The lid was lifted on the briefcase containing the nuclear codes. Within one minute, the necessary signals were entered, and the secret doors concealing over two hundred nuclear installations swung silently open. Seconds later, the sleek, slender missiles carrying their deadly payloads arched skyward.

The plan was to hit the areas containing the most highly concentrated number of enemy troops. Every target had been updated by the technicians who had worked throughout the night.

The first nuclear explosion hit the highway leading from Jericho to Jerusalem. It was one solid mass of enemy troops. When the blinding flash of the nuclear explosion was unleashed, the eyes of the enemy soldiers literally melted in their eye sockets. Tanks and half-tracks melted where they stood. Not one living thing was left within a ten-kilometer radius. Objects only a few kilometers away from the epicenter of the blast were hurled like pieces of straw through the air. Tanks even hurtled through the air for over a mile.

The different warheads swept swiftly to various targets in the Jordan Valley where enemy troops had been in total control for several days. The scene on the Jericho Road was repeated over and over as each missile unleashed its deadly destruction on the unsuspecting young pawns of the New World Order. Dead Russian troops lay everywhere.

With pinpoint precision, the Israeli missiles landed one by one, tracing the supply lines of Israel's enemies. Damascus, Syria, became one blazing inferno. Strangely, only one thing was left standing in Damascus—the famous Minaret of Jesus, one of the four minarets of the Mosques of Damascus. Interestingly, Muslims believe that Jesus will come back to earth, and that when He does, He will come to the Minaret of Jesus.

After the decision was made and the order given to use the Samson Option, there was only one thing for Prime Minister Alon to do. He went out to stand on the balcony. "Lord God, please grant favorable winds on the mountains of Israel at this time. Let the northwest winds blow. Let them carry death and destruction to those who would destroy Your people and banish Your name from the earth."

Alon felt the gentle breeze flowing through his hair. Assessing the direction of the wind, he knew they were not fighting alone. "Thank You, God," he whispered. "Thank You." He had never felt this close to God in his entire life! He knew better than anyone that, in spite of the Samson Option, Israel's situation was still desperate. Nevertheless, an inexplicable confidence was growing in his heart that, ultimately, everything would be all right.

They could not target the nuclear strikes too near to Jerusalem since radiation would have destroyed Israel's own troops. Consequently, the international community still had formidable forces within the ten-kilometer band that was left untouched by the Samson Option. Those forces, not fully realizing what was occurring throughout other parts of Israel, pressed forward toward the goal of occupying Jerusalem. And they were steadily gaining ground.

As the reports poured into Prime Minister Alon's command center, he wondered aloud, "Did we wait too long to trigger the Samson Option? Will all still be lost, in spite of the death and devastation we have wrought?"

On the front lines, the fighting was absolutely inhuman. The Global Forces had come around the side of the Mount of Olives and begun to bear down on the walls of the Temple Mount. The rumble of the tanks and the screaming of the jets overhead was deafening. The steady rat-a-tat-tat of five hundred machine guns never let up.

Men were dying by the thousands in the small Kidron Valley that separated the Mount of Olives from the Temple Mount. The command had been given that the holy places of Jerusalem were not to be bombed; consequently, the fighting was with small arms and hand grenades.

Wave after wave of New World Order soldiers dashed into the teeth of the deadly blanket of fire being laid down by Israeli sharpshooters positioned on the Temple Mount. So much blood had been shed that the soldiers were sloshing through it in their efforts to take the coveted Mount Moriah. One soldier lost his footing as he made his charge—and fell face down in the blood that had poured from the dead and dying. When he regained his footing, he was covered from head to toe with the blood of Armageddon.

Monte Ben-Isaac had served in the Israeli army for six years before Armageddon broke out. Because of his exceptional marksmanship and bravery under fire, he had been promoted to Israel's finest military unit. When it became obvious that war was inevitable, Monte's unit was assigned the sacred task of defending Jerusalem.

Monte had been fighting with almost no sleep since the invasion began. The weariness he felt as he pulled the trigger on his machine gun was bone-numbing. Yet he knew he would never give up as long as his ammunition held out. That was the one thing that worried him the most. Israel had been under an arms boycott for some time now. Some of her friends had secretly smuggled ammunition and weapons parts into the country. But would it be enough? They were facing an enemy with unlimited resources. Monte watched as the ammunition in the storage bins went steadily down.

"How's the ammo holding?" Monte asked his friend Ze'ev. Monte and Ze'ev had been best friends since their schooldays.

"It doesn't look good," Ze'ev replied. "The word is that we might have enough to last through today and part of tomorrow. Stretch it as far as you can."

But it was hard to worry about stretching bullets when you were fighting for your life every minute. After days of fighting, everything was now instinct. Monte sensed the next wave of enemy soldiers before he saw them. He knew the area he had to cover and the area that would be covered by the next Israeli positions on his right and on his left. When the marksman on his left ran out of ammo, he would put down a line of fire over that area, as well as his own, until he heard the rat-a-tat-tat pick up again. When his gun fell silent, his fellow soldiers returned the favor. And the blood in the Kidron Valley got deeper and deeper. The slaughter was absolutely horrible!

Monte really didn't know how he made it through that day, but finally dusk descended and gave way to night. The enemy dug in to wait for dawn, since they needed light for the hand-to-hand combat required for conquering Jerusalem. He was thankful for the reprieve, even though he knew full well that it was only temporary.

"You've got to get some sleep tonight, Monte," Ze'ev urged. "Israel is going to need you real bad tomorrow. I'll keep watch so you can rest."

It didn't take much insistence by Ze'ev for Monte to drop to the ground. Within seconds he was in a deep slumber. In his dreams all night he was killing—load another round into the machine gun—catch the next wave—stop them, we've got to stop them.

Monte didn't know what awakened him, but he bolted straight up. What time was it? He looked at his watch. Four a.m....about one hour before the assault would begin again. Ze'ev spoke from where he was sitting about ten feet away. "You all right?"

"Sure," Monte quickly replied. "How's the ammunition?" He saw the troubled look on Ze'ev's face.

"It's not good," his friend admitted. "As a matter of fact, it's pretty bad."

"How long can we last?" Monte asked anxiously. "I knew we were getting low last night."

Ze'ev shook his head. "Five hours, maybe six, if we're lucky."

"Can we borrow some from another unit? Are there new supplies on the way?" Monte asked with increasing apprehension.

"Everyone is in the same shape as we are. There are no new supplies. Unless God performs a miracle, we're finished," Ze'ev reported.

"Ze'ev, it can't end like this!" Monte protested. "This can't be what God has in mind for His land. He brought us from all the nations of the world and miraculously established us in this land. You know that the prophecy of Ezekiel doesn't end with our annihilation. It ends with Israel as a light to the nations."

Ze'ev looked his friend straight in the eye, "I know, Monte. But if we are to resist the forces of the New World Order, God is simply going to have to intervene. We've run out of answers."

Monte and Ze'ev simultaneously dropped to their knees, and together they prayed, "O God, this is Your land, and Jerusalem is the place where You said You would place Your name. Now, Lord, we've done the best that we could do, but still we stand this morning on the brink of defeat. We don't know how You could turn the tide of this dismal situation, but we know You can do it. Help us now, O God, we pray. We are in Your hands. Amen."

Ze'ev and Monte positioned their guns and their ammunition in preparation for the assault they knew would come at any moment. Before the World Community pierced the defenses of Jerusalem through their position, the enemy would pay a high price.

Monte sensed movement to his right. "Here they come," he shouted. He and Ze'ev laid down a deadly blanket of fire that consumed every human being in its path. As the charging soldiers were cut in two by the deadly barrage, their eyes would roll backwards as their bodies contorted in the throes of death. It was a hellish sight!

The charge of the Global Forces continued unabated for six solid hours. Several thousand bodies now completely covered the floor of the Kidron. Still the Israeli forces held. As the UN troops regrouped, Ze'ev did a quick inventory of their ammunition. His report wasn't good. "We might have enough to last one more hour."

When the charge resumed, it was with terrible fury. Monte believed they could hold if only they had ammunition. But when he looked in the ammo box, he estimated they had no more than 15 minutes worth of supply left. Well, if they were going down, they would resist to the last bullet.

The dread of what was coming and the cumulative tiredness of the last nine days weighed heavily on Monte's shoulders. In his weariness, he leaned against the stones of the Temple Mount walls. As he lifted his eyes, he saw, for what he knew might be the last time, the beautiful Mount of Olives. His mother had taught him that when Messiah came, He would come to that place. Lifting his eyes in desperation to the skies above the Mount of Olives, he prayed fervently, "Messiah, if You're ever going to come, You've got to come now!"

Monte reloaded his machine gun and resumed firing. The roar of the tanks, the throb of the rotor blades from the helicopters, and the rat-a-tat-tat from the machine guns drowned out everything else. It was impossible to communicate now except with one's eyes. But there was no need. Both Ze'ev and Monte knew the moment of truth was at hand.

Monte's gun fell silent, indicating that it was time to reload. When he grabbed the belt of ammunition from the ammo box, he noticed it was the last one. He slapped the ammunition into place and resumed his position behind the sights. *I've got to make this last one count*, he thought to himself. Ze'ev and Monte were exacting a terrible price from the enemy, but still they came. Days of non-stop fighting had taught Monte to sense when the last few bullets were entering the chamber. He could tell that time had now come. "O, God help us," he silently prayed.

When his gun fell silent, his mind raced furiously. *What do we do now?* His fellow soldiers all the way down the line of defense were going through the same thing he and Ze'ev were experiencing. One by one, the guns fell silent.

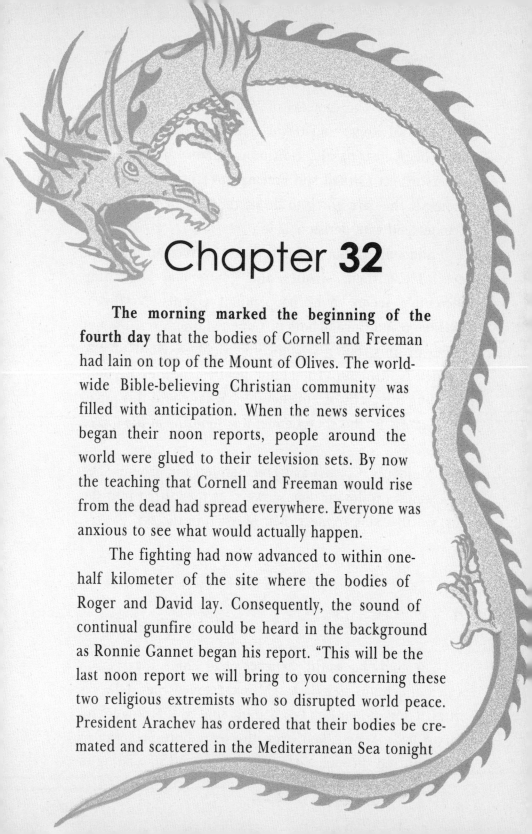

Chapter 32

The morning marked the beginning of the fourth day that the bodies of Cornell and Freeman had lain on top of the Mount of Olives. The worldwide Bible-believing Christian community was filled with anticipation. When the news services began their noon reports, people around the world were glued to their television sets. By now the teaching that Cornell and Freeman would rise from the dead had spread everywhere. Everyone was anxious to see what would actually happen.

The fighting had now advanced to within one-half kilometer of the site where the bodies of Roger and David lay. Consequently, the sound of continual gunfire could be heard in the background as Ronnie Gannet began his report. "This will be the last noon report we will bring to you concerning these two religious extremists who so disrupted world peace. President Arachev has ordered that their bodies be cremated and scattered in the Mediterranean Sea tonight at midnight." The cameras of WNN zoomed in close on the faces of Roger and David as Gannet continued. "We have been hearing the ridiculous rumor that the End-timers expect Cornell and Freeman to rise from the dead today. If they are going to do it, they had better hurry," Gannet said with derision.

Suddenly Gannet thought he saw Freeman blink his eyes. He gasped. "Ladies and gentlemen, something incredible seems to be happening," Gannet exclaimed. "Freeman and Cornell both just opened their eyes! I'm not believing this, but it's happening right in front of me. Cornell is sitting up. Ladies and gentlemen, they are both standing now! This is unbelievable! What could this possibly mean?!" By this time Gannet was shouting at the top of his voice.

Suddenly, Cornell and Freeman left the ground. The TV cameras followed them upward as they lifted into the air, swiftly rising to meet their Messiah in the sky.

Around the world, believers had come together to catch the noon newscast. The expectancy they felt was electrifying. When Ron Gannet announced that Roger and David had opened their eyes, the incredible presence of God coursed through each of them. Instead of abating in a few moments, as God's presence usually did, it continued to increase until it felt like white lightning flowing through each of their veins. The ecstasy that the power of God's presence produced in them approached the limits of human endurance.

Charles and Anna Rhodes had been Christians for 20 years. As they listened to the newscast, they held hands in intense expectation. Suddenly, in the throes of divine ecstasy, they felt the floor receding beneath their feet. As they passed through the ceiling along with the other believers, a great shout of praise came from the depths of their beings. They were on their way to meet their Savior in the air!

As Charles floated upward through the sky, his eyes began to search among the clouds that floated overhead. Then he saw Him. Standing on a cloud silhouetted against the blue sky was the One he had worshiped all these years. Suddenly, he found himself shouting, "Jesus, Jesus!" The sensation was beyond anything humanly possible. It was as though he was being pulled into a whirlpool of love. The peace and the purity of the feeling was sublime.

The journey upward continued until Charles found himself kneeling at Jesus' feet. Warm tears of love streamed down his now immortal face as he praised his Savior and Creator for His wonderful salvation. Charles found that all he could say was, "I love You. I love You. I love You."

The amazing thing about all of this was that every one who had been caught up was experiencing the same thing simultaneously. Since the laws of space no longer existed in this immortal dimension, every person could be just as close to Jesus as the other. Now, all unanswered questions were answered. Every raptured saint was incorporated into the mind of God, and the level of enlightenment and understanding encompassed the entirety of history and the universe. For the first time, Charles understood First Corinthians 13:12: "For now we see through a glass, darkly; but then face to face: now I know in part; but then shall I know even as also I am known."

Charles had no sense of how long this particular experience continued, nor did he care. He was utterly bathed in the effervescent presence of Almighty God. It was glorious!

As this meeting in the air continued, every person present understood his particular part in the Kingdom of God. They did not have to be told. It was as if they each had been grafted into the mind of Jesus so that His thoughts were now their thoughts. They dwelled in a state of perfect union with their Lord and Savior. And they all knew that the time had come to visit the Mount of Olives.

Chapter **33**

For a brief moment, when the Israeli guns fell silent, the cessation of firing disconcerted the enemy, causing the advance to stop. Then the Global Forces seized the opportunity and surged forward like a tidal wave all the way up and down the Kidron. "God help us!" Monte cried in desperation as he watched the advance troops rush the Temple Mount walls. The portable ladders clanged against the city walls even as enemy helicopters swooped down to land on the now defenseless Temple Mount.

At that very moment, a glowing brightness appeared on the eastern horizon, just over the Mount of Olives. Monte felt the hair on his arms begin to stand on end. He had heard people say that was what they experienced just before the touchdown of a tornado. *What is going on?* Monte's mind raced. *Maybe our government has a new secret weapon that nobody knows about.* The brightness steadily increased in intensity as it grew closer and closer. Could it be...?

By now Monte had forgotten about the critical danger he was in. The approaching light began to take on shape and form. It was almost like an invasion from the sky by extraterrestrial forces. Then he saw horses—dazzling white horses. Their riders appeared to be clothed in light. Monte's eyes locked on the front horse and rider who was larger and more brilliant than the rest.

"My Lord and my God!" Monte exclaimed. "This is our Messiah! Ze'ev, our Messiah has come!"

Monte was not the only one distracted by the invasion from the skies. The soldiers of the New World army occupying the Mount of Olives whirled to face this new enemy descending from the sky. Tanks, helicopters, and machine guns filled the air with a fusilade of bullets. But this celestial force continued its descent onto the Mount of Olives undeterred. The brightness of Messiah and His saints became blinding. Global soldiers dropped their weapons while attempting to shield their eyes from the incredible white light. The brightness was so overwhelming that men fell to the ground before the force of it.

"Ze'ev, I'm going to meet Him," Monte announced.

"I'm with you. Let's go!" Ze'ev shouted.

All the tiredness of the past days fled from Monte's body. His heart pumped with newfound adrenaline as he ran at full speed through the bodies scattered over the Kidron Valley. He and Ze'ev ran, side by side, up the

Mount of Olives toward the place where their Messiah had landed.

Strangely, the overwhelming light seemed to have melted into peace. Monte noticed that hundreds, perhaps thousands, of other Jews were running toward their Messiah as well. Apparently, they, too, understood what was happening.

Monte and Ze'ev were among the first to reach the white-clad figure who had dismounted and stood waiting for them. They both fell at His feet in adoration. "Messiah! O Messiah! You came just in time! Thank You. We love You."

Messiah didn't have to say a word in return. They knew He loved them. It was as though liquid love flowed out from Him, overwhelming all who were near. His presence was transforming every single person who bowed to worship Him.

Monte brushed the tears from his eyes, finally daring to look upward into his Messiah's face. Messiah's eyes met his and, at that moment, Monte's Messiah reached His hand out to him. Something about the gesture temporarily distracted Monte. It was the hands. There were scars in His hands.

Monte spoke before he realized what he was doing. "Messiah, where did You get these wounds?" Even as he asked the question, Monte knew what the answer would be.

"I received these in the house of My friends." The reply was without bitterness or hatred—just a simple statement.

Then Monte understood everything. Now it all made sense. "So You're Jesus?" he inquired.

"I'm Jesus," came the affirmative reply.

"O Messiah, we have been so blind! We have been so stubborn! O Messiah, could You ever forgive us?" By now Monte was weeping uncontrollably. But even in his repentance he felt the love emanating from Jesus. Jesus took him by the arm, raising him to his feet. Monte couldn't explain it, but he knew beyond all doubt that he was forgiven totally and completely.

> *And one shall say unto Him, What are these wounds in Thine hands? Then He shall answer, Those with which I was wounded in the house of My friends.* Zechariah 13:6

> *...blindness in part is happened to Israel, until the fulness of the Gentiles be come in. And so all Israel shall be saved...* Romans 11:25-26

Understanding
the Endtime

Level One

Bible prophecy series authored by

Irvin Baxter

Ten Lessons
1. United States & Other Modern Nations in the Bible
2. New World Order Is World Government
3. Mideast Peace—Prelude to Armageddon
4. The Four Horsemen
5. The Roman Empire Revived
6. Antichrist & False Prophet
7. Mark of the Beast
8. The Coming One-World Religion
9. How to Enter the Kingdom of God
10. The Rapture

Three ways to learn
Video Series • Cassette Series • Study Manual
Four Ways to Teach
Flip Chart • Transparencies • Slides • Video Series

You will understand prophecy like never before!

www.endtime.com

Deadly Intentions: Inside the Mind of the Antichrist

In his coming book, *Deadly Intentions: Inside the Mind of the Antichrist*, author Irvin Baxter gets inside the head of Antichrist Arachev. What experiences of childhood could result in such incredible brilliance and yet such spiritual darkness? How does a human being actually come to believe that he has been chosen to be the world's savior, the Messiah?

Deadly Intentions: Inside the Mind of the Antichrist will explore dark alleys of the antichrist's mind as he weaves his diabolical plan for world domination. How does a human being enslave and destroy so many, all in the name of peace? More importantly, how does he dupe the masses of the world to give him their faith and allegiance?

You will understand the forces of globalization that are presently engulfing our world and you will see how you fit into the antichrist's scheme, once you have read *Deadly Intentions: Inside the Mind of the Antichrist*.

Excerpt:

As the crowd chanted, "Arachev, Messiah. Arachev, Messiah," Moshe looked on in amazement. His emotions exploded into shocking horror when Pope Peter II swept his white robed arm toward Arachev, "The world's long-awaited Messiah. Receive him!"

Louder than ever, the chant resumed, "Arachev, Messiah. Arachev, Messiah. Pope Peter II is his prophet. Pope Peter II is Elijah!" The crowd began to clap in rhythm as they chanted. Soon thousands of people were chanting, clapping, and stomping their feet. The rising crescendo of the chant was utterly enthralling. The scene was captivatingly euphoric as it engulfed the crowd, sucking almost every person on the Temple Mount into its vibrating vortex.

Moshe looked on in stunned fascination and horror. "Is there any truth to these incredible revelations? Surely not! But where will all this lead?" Moshe had lived long enough to recognize the birth of a mass movement. He also was certain that the day's developments were not as spontaneous as they appeared. This entire charade had certainly been orchestrated. How masterful the manipulation had been!

Where would all this lead? As Moshe pondered the day's events, searching in his mind for answers, one thing became obvious to him. The world was being led by a well-thought-out plan. The forces sweeping the world into the arms of Michael Arachev were not a spontaneous phenomenon.

But what was the plan? He must understand what was going on if he was to resist the force of this global movement and warn others. But how could he? It was all so confusing!

A thought was slowly emerging in his mind as to where he might find his answers. He needed to learn about Michael Arachev. The man was a master manipulator. If he could understand the power that had shaped the man, then he would understand the plan.

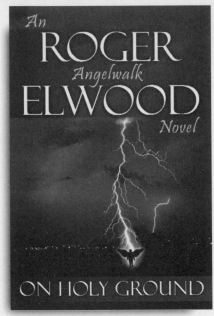

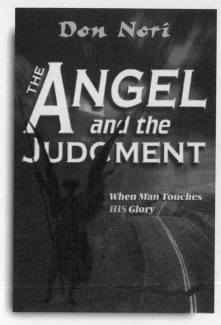

ISBN: 1-56043-154-7

THE ANGEL AND THE JUDGMENT

By Don Nori

Few understand the power of our judgments, or the aftermath of the words we speak in thoughtless, emotional pain. In this powerful story about a preacher and an angel, you'll see how the heavens respond and how the earth is changed by the words we utter in secret.

THE NEW AMPLIFIED PILGRIM'S PROGRESS

By John Bunyan

John Bunyan's amazing *Pilgrim's Progress* is well into its fourth century of unparalleled popularity as the world's best-selling non-biblical book in all history. Now in modern English comes *The New Amplified Pilgrim's Progress*. All the age-old spiritual treasures of John Bunyan's original are now carried to new heights of power and clarity in this new enhanced version. While this is perhaps the most adventure-filled and user-friendly adaptation ever penned, yet it is totally unabridged and, excepting certain amplified scenes, remains strictly faithful to Bunyan's original storyline.

Exciting new levels of love and joy, hope and humor are skillfully woven by master storyteller Jim Pappas, into this enchanting retelling of John Bunyan's immortal classic! Designed to return this spellbinding masterpiece of angels and giants, castles and dragon, to the fireside of the everyday reader.

ISBN: 0-7684-2051-2

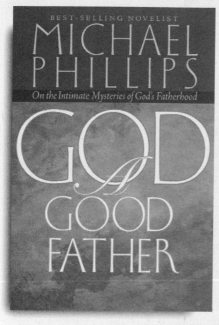

GOD: A GOOD FATHER

By Michael Phillips

In this startling book, Michael Phillips challenges the established Christian to step out of the status quo and into a breathtaking new relationship with God the Father. In a style reminiscent of John Bunyan's classic *Pilgrim's Progress*, Phillips acts as a "guide" on a journey to the place of the presence of our Heavenly Father.

A "divine restlessness" will stir your heart as you follow Michael Phillips out of the "fogbound lowlands" of our typical existence and you climb to the "mountain home of *Abba* Father," learning to know Him—His love, His goodness, His trustworthiness, His forgiveness—and choosing to live in His heart and drink of His water of life forever!

ISBN: 0-7684-2123-3

Additional copies of this book and other
book titles from DESTINY IMAGE are
available at your local bookstore.

For a complete list of our titles,
visit us at www.destinyimage.com
Send a request for a catalog to:

Destiny Image₍ᵣ₎ Publishers, Inc.
P.O. Box 310
Shippensburg, PA 17257-0310

*"Speaking to the Purposes of God for This
Generation and for the Generations to Come"*